INSIDE HUDSON PICKLE

The author is grateful for support from the Canada Council for the Arts. She also wishes to thank her critique partners (David Wright, Eileen Feldsott, Lawrence Tabak, Miriam Spitzer Franklin), Sara Wienke of The Alpha-1 Center, Amy Tompkins, Jennifer MacKinnon, and the amazing team at Kids Can Press.

❥ ❥ ❥

KCP Fiction is an imprint of Kids Can Press

Text © 2017 Yolanda Ridge

Kids Can Press gratefully acknowledges the financial support of the Government of Ontario, through the Ontario Media Development Corporation; the Ontario Arts Council; the Canada Council for the Arts; and the Government of Canada, through the CBF, for our publishing activity.

Published in Canada and the U.S. by Kids Can Press Ltd.
25 Dockside Drive, Toronto, ON M5A 0B5

Kids Can Press is a Corus Entertainment Inc. company

www.kidscanpress.com

Edited by Jennifer Mackinnon
Designed by Marie Bartholomew
Cover illustration by Vidhya Nagarajan

Manufactured in Shenzhen, China, in 3/2017 by C & C Offset

CM 17 0 9 8 7 6 5 4 3 2 1

Library and Archives Canada Cataloguing in Publication

Ridge, Yolanda, 1973–, author
   Inside Hudson Pickle / written by Yolanda Ridge.
ISBN 978-1-77138-620-3 (hardback)
      I. Title.
PS8635.I374I58 2017   jC813'.6   C2016-906542-1

INSIDE HUDSON PICKLE

YOLANDA RIDGE

KCP Fiction

CHAPTER ONE

"Hudson! We're going out!" The panic in my mom's voice cut through my bedroom door like a right winger splitting the defense.

I glanced at the clock. Mom should still be cleaning up from dinner and packing lunches for tomorrow. I tossed my *Sports Illustrated* on the floor.

"What are you talking about?" I yelled back. "I'm doing my homework!"

The bedroom door burst open. Mom's shiny red face appeared. "There's been a fire," she said. "Get your coat."

I felt a kick of adrenaline, the kind I used to get when Coach called my name for the starting lineup. "Fire?"

"It's Uncle Vic," Mom said, her voice quavering.

I rolled off the bed, thinking, *This could be good.* Excitement followed Uncle Vic like stink follows gym socks.

Was it another one of his stunts? This one time

he'd sat in a tree and played his guitar for forty-eight hours straight to protest clear-cut logging. He'd gotten a lot of attention for that one, thanks to a video that went viral.

Or it could be something even crazier, like a run-in with the law. Uncle Vic had served time as a teenager, though I'd never gotten a straight answer on why. He'd also been arrested for disturbing the peace and obstruction of justice. I only know about that because I'd read it in the newspaper. It was stuck in the back pages of the entertainment section where they bury news about pseudo-famous local people.

Nothing was too out there when it came to Uncle Vic, but he didn't strike me as an arsonist.

"For real? A fire?" I asked.

"Yes, a real fire." Mom exhaled hard, making her long blond bangs fan out like an umbrella. "And, yes, your uncle is fine."

"Oh, right." It hadn't occurred to me that Uncle Vic might be hurt. The guy was invincible. "So what's the panic?"

"We'll talk in the car." Mom was already bundled up in the oversize down jacket she'd been wearing since Labor Day.

I grabbed my hoodie off the floor and followed her to the garage.

"Calm down, Mom," I said as she backed out of the driveway at twice her normal speed. Her normal speed was painfully slow, but still, she was starting to freak me out. "What's going on?"

"I don't really know. Vic just called and said there'd been a fire. He asked me to come and get him."

"A fire in his apartment?" Uncle Vic lived in a basement apartment near the center of town, miles away from our square box in the 'burbs.

"Yes, in his apartment," Mom replied, her eyes fixed on the straight, flat road ahead.

"How'd it happen?"

"He put the kettle on and then fell asleep." She gripped the steering wheel so tight her knuckles looked like they were about to burst out of her black leather gloves. "That's all I know, Hudson. We'll find out the rest when we get there."

I slouched into the seat and turned on the radio. The droning twang of Mom's country music station filled the car. "The hockey game should be on." I fiddled with the controls. "It's already started ..."

"Just keep it low," Mom said without taking her eyes off the road.

"Fine."

She drove to Uncle Vic's place like she was racing

in the Indy 500. I kept glancing at the speedometer as I tried to concentrate on the play-by-play.

A rookie fumbled a pass.

Another player went offside on what sounded like an easy breakaway.

I gritted my teeth, wishing I could stream the NHL preseason. Instead, I was stuck listening to one of the many varsity games that flooded the airwaves in this hockey-crazed town. My jaw clenched even harder as the commentator announced a line change. When would I stop imagining the sound of my own name floating over the radio waves?

Pickle shoots ... He scores!

Never going to happen.

•••

When we arrived at Uncle Vic's, Mom had to park a block away — an obvious sign that something big was going down. In the sprawling town of Bluster, tucked away in the least populated county of Western New York, you never have to park a block away from anything, ever.

As I ducked out of the car, the foul smell of burning, wet wood and melted plastic hit me like a punch. It reminded me of the time Trev and I had torched our collection of Star Wars action figures.

They hadn't gone up in flames, but they'd bubbled and then melted, producing dark trails of smoke. That had triggered an asthma attack major enough to put me in the hospital — which was the only thing that had saved me from being grounded for a year.

Fire trucks, police cars and ambulances crowded the road in front of Uncle Vic's, blocking my view of the house. I looked up but couldn't see any flames — just clouds of smoke and steam reflecting the flashing yellow and red lights of the emergency vehicles. The sirens were silent.

Pulling my hood around my neck so it covered my nose and mouth, I took a breath and rushed to catch up with Mom. The last thing I needed was an asthma attack. *Childhood* asthma was supposed to disappear now that I had officially entered my teenage years. But if anyone was going to beat the odds — the odds of something bad happening, that is, not something good — it would be me.

"You okay?" Mom asked as I stepped up beside her.

"Yeah," I mumbled through the fabric, even though my chest didn't feel right. It was tight. Asthma-attack tight. I felt the pocket of my hoodie for an inhaler. Nothing.

She stopped. "Maybe you should wait in the car."

"I'm fine." I grabbed her arm and dragged her up the street. "Let's just find Uncle Vic."

We found him sitting in the back of an ambulance. With one hand, he held an oxygen mask up to his face. The other hand held together the ends of a blanket, which was wrapped haphazardly around his shoulders. His legs were bare, and his feet dangled above the ground like a little kid's in a grown-up chair.

"Oh my god, Vic," Mom said when she saw him. "You must be frozen."

Uncle Vic lifted the mask away from his scruffy goatee and smiled. "I'm fine, sis. Like I told you on the phone."

"Yes, but ..." Mom glanced at the old Victorian house across the road. "I didn't expect so much ... damage."

The tightness in my chest slowly started to relax its grip as I stared at the house. A floodlight from one of the fire trucks made the place look like a Halloween haunted house. Smoke billowed out the windows and rose up from the pointed roof. The wooden slats on the sides of the house, once flat and blue, now looked like charred campfire logs.

"Hey, kid," said Uncle Vic. "Thanks for coming."

"Yeah, sure," I said casually, even though I was kind of psyched to be there. I know it's twisted, but being at the scene of a fire was exciting. Much more exciting than a night at home: me upstairs, watching hockey on my laptop while playing Minecraft on my tablet, and Mom downstairs, muttering at the TV as if the characters on *Downton Abbey* could actually hear her.

A paramedic appeared from inside the ambulance and took the oxygen mask from Uncle Vic. "Breathing okay?" she asked.

"Better," he replied.

"I'm going to check your vitals one more time," she said.

While the paramedic took Uncle Vic's temperature and blood pressure, I watched firefighters move in and out of the house with hoses, axes and a bunch of equipment I didn't recognize. I'd been fascinated by firefighters as a kid. What they were doing seemed a lot more interesting than standing around on the sidelines like a pylon.

Uncle Vic coughed a loud, rumbling cough, as though lava was going to come exploding out of him. It was a cough I recognized.

"I think we better take you in," the paramedic said as she pulled out her stethoscope.

"I don't need to go to the hospital," Uncle Vic said, trying to catch his breath. "I have coughing fits all the time. It has nothing to do with the fire."

"Are you a smoker?"

"Not anymore."

The paramedic pushed her stethoscope under the folds of his blanket and listened to his chest and back. "Your lungs sound crackly. Have you had a respiratory infection lately?"

"No. I mean ... yeah."

"You had a cold?" asked Mom. "When?"

"Last week. My nose was running like a tap. And my throat was so hoarse I ended a gig after a single set — even though my fans seemed to think I sounded sexier than ever." Uncle Vic winked at the paramedic.

"There must be something nasty going around," Mom said. "Hudson's been sick, too."

"If it was upper respiratory, your lungs should be clear." The paramedic frowned. "It could be the smoke —"

"I feel fine, really, and I don't want to see any doctors." Uncle Vic put his hand on the paramedic's arm. "My sister works at the hospital. I'm going home with her. She'll keep an eye on me."

The paramedic looked at Mom. "His vitals are

good. He's stable so I can release him to you. But I think he should get checked out if that cough doesn't clear up soon."

"I'm just an ultrasound tech," Mom said. "But I work at Mercy General. I'll make sure he gets a thorough examination."

"Thanks, sis." Uncle Vic turned to me. "Looks like you have a new bunkmate, kid."

A shiver of excitement ran down my spine. Having Uncle Vic around would certainly stir things up — and take a little of Mom's overprotective attention away from me.

Mom sighed. "It'll be a bit of a squeeze ..."

A deep voice interrupted her. "Excuse me? Mr. Pickle?" It was one of the firefighters. He wore full protective gear and a large oxygen tank on his back. Black soot covered his face, blending in with the tight, dark curls on his head. "Are you Victor Pickle?"

"In the flesh," said Uncle Vic.

"Sorry to meet you under these unfortunate circumstances." The firefighter pulled off his right glove. "E. O. Bouchier."

Uncle Vic shook the firefighter's hand enthusiastically. "What can I do for you?"

"I'm here to give you an update. The county fire department accomplished fire control within approximately fifty minutes of being on the scene." He paused to consult the clipboard he had tucked under the left arm of his bulky jacket. "Sixty-three minutes after your upstairs neighbor made the 9-1-1 call. Everyone was evacuated, and no one sustained significant injury."

Uncle Vic raised his eyebrows. "That's good, right?"

The firefighter cleared his throat. "Yes. But the damage is extensive. I'm afraid you won't be able to return home for a while." He handed Uncle Vic a business card and confirmed his contact information. "We'll be in touch. This your family here?"

Uncle Vic nodded.

The firefighter acknowledged me with a smile. "It must be hard to see your dad in this situation."

"He's not my dad," I blurted out, startled by the assumption. It's true that Uncle Vic was the closest thing I had to a dad. Still, the thought of him being some kind of father figure was absurd. He might be old enough, but he definitely wasn't mature enough. And besides that, we looked absolutely nothing alike. "Definitely not my dad," I repeated, shaking my head for emphasis.

"I'm sorry. I just —"

Mom jumped in before the firefighter could consult his clipboard again. "He's my brother. Hudson's uncle. We're all the family he has here. He'll be staying with us."

"It's lucky he has a place to go to. The homeowners have insurance, but it might not cover tenants." He glanced over at a couple with three young kids, huddled together next to a police car. I recognized them as the family who lived upstairs.

Mom glared at Uncle Vic. "Don't you have your own insurance?"

He ignored her. "Can I go in and get some stuff?"

"Not yet. I'll be in touch to let you know when it's safe." The firefighter flipped down the face shield attached to his red helmet. Case closed.

"Okay." Uncle Vic hopped out of the ambulance. As he did, the blanket slid off his shoulders.

The firefighter turned away.

Mom gasped.

I bit my lip to stop from laughing.

Uncle Vic was wearing nothing but his underwear.

And I'm not talking boxers.

CHAPTER TWO

"Hudson Pickle?"

My back stiffened on reflex. Tearing my eyes away from the window, I faced the front of the classroom.

"Hudson?" Ms. Lavender repeated. "Are you with us?"

It took me a second to remember what class I was in. Career & Tech. Right. "Of course," I lied. It's not like I could tell her that replaying the scene of last night's fire was at least a billion times more interesting than her lesson. Who cares about choosing the right career in seventh grade?

"Then answer the question," said Ms. Lavender.

I swallowed. "Question?"

"Your profession?"

I still wasn't sure what she wanted, so I just said the first thing that popped into my head. "Firefighter."

A tinkering of laughter drifted forward from the back of the room. What had I gotten myself into?

"Very well." Ms. Lavender wrote something on her clipboard. "Anyone else? Willow Flores?"

I ducked down so the rest of my row could see over my head again. Not that anyone was looking at Ms. Lavender. All eyes were glued on Willow, who sat at attention in the desk next to mine.

"I can't decide between mail carrier and sports broadcaster," Willow answered.

More laughter from the back of the room.

Ms. Lavender sighed. "Those are two very different professions, Willow."

"You want to be a *mailman*?" said Aidan Pace. I could tell it was him, even though he was sitting behind me with the other eighth-grade boys, who were now laughing harder than ever. "Willow can't be a mail*man*, even if she is the tallest girl to ever live."

"That's enough, Aidan."

"But Ms. Lavender, I'm just thinking of Willow. If she becomes a mailman, it might make her crazy. It might make her go *postal* or something."

"Aidan ..."

Willow crossed her arms over her chest. "Mail carrier it is, Ms. Lavender."

I watched Willow out of the corner of my eye. She kept her chin pointed forward, jaw set. I knew that look on her face: determination. I knew it from the board games we'd played in kindergarten and our rounds of tag at recess. I knew it from the face-offs we'd taken against each other in house league. Of course, all of that was before I moved up a level in hockey and down a grade in school.

I didn't really know Willow anymore. But she was obviously the same girl who'd sunk my battleship and captured my snow fort. Gutsy move, standing up to Aidan like that.

♥♥♥

"Hey! Wait up!" I called to Trev when the bell finally rang, putting an end to Career & Tech and the school day.

Trev didn't slow down as he filed out of the classroom ahead of me. Not that I'd really expected him to.

"Not cool, Hudson," he hissed when I finally caught up to him. "You need to pay attention. Those eighth graders are always looking for a reason to rip seventh graders apart. You're lucky Aidan didn't pick on you instead of Willow."

"Wait for me at your locker so we can walk home together," I said. "You need to fill me in on what I missed."

"I don't need to do anything." Trev shook his head.

"You missed the assignment? That's your problem. I'm not hanging around."

"But —" I started to protest, even though it was obviously a waste of time. Trev was never going to forgive me for the way I'd treated him last year, and I didn't really blame him. I'd been a chump. A world-class, first-rate chump. And I'd been so blinded by hockey that I hadn't even noticed.

Trev sped ahead as I stopped in front of my locker. I spun the lock, trying to remember the combination. I flipped it up in frustration when it refused to open. Twisting the dial back to zero, I tried a couple more times, then finally gave up. Mom would be mad if I didn't bring home my lunch bag, but I couldn't stand the thought of people staring at me — the tall, gangly seventh grader who couldn't even win a battle against his own locker.

I took off down the hallway, weaving through groups of giggling kids I didn't recognize, and passed by Trev's locker without slowing down. He was already gone. I scanned the hall for a glimpse of his fiery red hair — nothing. With a sigh, I headed toward the door, all set to walk home alone. Again.

But as the hallway cleared in front of me, I caught a glimpse of Trev. He was rushing toward the exit. Walking quickly. Head forward. Back straight.

And then suddenly he was down, sprawled on the floor. His books, his pens, his lunch bag, his open backpack scattered in every direction, like equipment on the ice after a hockey brawl.

I hurried up to Trev while Aidan and his friends gathered around him, their laughter echoing off the lockers. I could tell Aidan had tripped Trev — you didn't need to see the play to know when someone had drawn a penalty.

Trev scrambled to pick up all the stuff off the floor. I got down on my hands and knees to help.

When everything was back in his backpack, or stuffed into our pockets, we hurried to our feet and tried to walk away. But Aidan kept dekeing in front of Trev, blocking him in every direction. "Who are you?" he finally demanded, as if they hadn't sat in the same Career & Tech class for the last month.

Trev responded in the tiniest voice I'd ever heard, "Trevor Bach."

"Elmo and his buddy Big Bird is more like it." Aidan smirked at his friends before turning back to Trev. "You're a long way from Sesame Street, dudes. Can you walk down the hall without falling, or do you need help from your mommy?"

Trev didn't react — exactly the right thing to do according to the antibullying lecture we'd had in elementary school. But Trev had a black belt in karate. Shouldn't that have given him the confidence to stand up for himself? To make a statement, so he didn't end up with a target on his back at the beginning of junior high?

"Shut up, Aidan," I hissed in the deepest voice I could muster.

He narrowed his eyes at me, taking in my height and my skinny, pathetic arms. "Is Big Bird your bodyguard, Trevor Bach?"

"No, I'm his friend." I glanced at Aidan's crew. I knew a couple of them from hockey. "Hey, Matthew," I said, nodding to the captain of my old peewee team.

Matthew looked at me, confused. Not because he didn't recognize me, but because he couldn't decide what to do.

I turned to my other old teammate, desperate for some acknowledgment. "Liam, buddy ..." The seconds ticked by in slow motion. I silently urged him to bump my fist, which hung between us like a rotten apple on a branch. "It's been a while —" My voice cracked. I stopped talking and dropped my fist.

All five of them collapsed into fits of laughter, Matthew and Liam included.

"We don't hang around with little kids," Aidan

snickered. "You and Trevor Bach better fly on out of here." Aidan flapped his arms like a chicken and clucked, "Bawk, bawk, bawk, bawk, ba-WK!"

The rest of the guys joined in, squawking, strutting and flapping like lunatics.

Trev tightened the straps of his backpack as he hurried toward the exit. Head hanging. Back slumped.

I glared at Aidan.

He took a step forward.

I backed down. Without another word, I followed Trev.

I wasn't a fighter — especially when no one had my back.

♥♥♥

I caught up with Trev in the back alley. It wasn't like I was trying to follow him. It's just that the alley was empty (of people, not garbage), and my legs were about twice as long as his.

I fell into step with him, and we walked home in silence. I don't know what was going through Trev's mind, but here's what I was thinking: *jerk, jerk, jerk, jerk, JERK*. It ran through my head to the rhythm of Aidan's chicken chant. Two jerks for Aidan, one for Matthew, one for Liam and a big one for me. For deserting Trev last year.

The story with him is kind of like the story with Willow, but instead of drifting apart we'd been ripped and torn.

Trev and I had been tight in a way that only next-door neighbors six months apart in age can be. Our friendship took a hit when I started school ahead of him — the curse of being born in December. But that hadn't lasted long, thanks to my repeat run through second grade.

Things were cool between us until last year when I started ditching Trev for hockey more and more. Then I'd made a choice that blew it all to smithereens.

Trev had been competing in the New York State Martial Arts Tournament being held right here in Bluster. Instead of going to watch, which I knew he wanted me to, I'd bowed out because of hockey. Not just for one of his bouts but for all of them. And not for an important game, just the regular set of early-season weekend practices. But here's the clincher: instead of coming clean, I'd lied and told him my grandma was sick — a lie that had popped like a blister when his gran had asked my mom about Grandma's recovery.

I didn't blame him for hating me. Even I hated me.

"This doesn't change anything, Hudson," Trev said when we'd finally reached the cul-de-sac where our houses stood, side by side, like mirror images of each other.

"What do you mean?"

Trev pulled the brim of his cap down over his almost-nonexistent orange eyebrows. "I don't need your protection."

"I don't want to protect you. I just —"

"You just need someone to eat lunch with?"

"Well —"

"Sorry there wasn't a welcome sign waiting for you at the jock table, but ..." Trev's voice trailed off as he lifted his cap and wiped his forehead with the back of his hand. "It's not my problem."

"Well ..." I repeated slowly, embarrassed by my string of lonely library lunches. Trev was right on that score. I'd been shunned by my eighth- and ninth-grade teammates — make that ex-teammates — on the very first day of school. Partly because none of them would be caught dead eating lunch with a lowly seventh grader, but also because I was no longer part of the team.

All of the other seventh graders had balled together like wads of old hockey tape — everyone but me. After all the time I'd spent on the ice with the older kids, missing birthday parties and after-school activities, I wasn't tight enough with any of them to stick. I guess for Trev, it was payback. He'd refused to offer me a spot at his table of gamers.

"Can you just give me the lowdown on Career and Tech?" I asked.

"What's the deal with firefighting anyway?" Trev scoffed. "I thought you gave that up years ago."

"And I thought you'd given up on ..." I couldn't think of a comeback. Trev had picked video-game developer for the Career & Tech project. It was what he'd wanted to be for as long as I could remember, and I knew it would never change.

As we stood there staring at each other, my first-grade trip to the fire station flashed through my mind. I'd really wanted to be a firefighter back then. Not in that cute little-kid way where everyone wants to be a superhero or a princess. No, becoming a firefighter had been my long-term plan, and Mom had totally encouraged it — easiest Halloween costume ever, she'd said. For years I'd dressed up in my oversize hard hat, rubber boots and reflective jacket (and not just for Halloween). And Trev had always been my ninja sidekick.

"There was a fire at my uncle's last night," I said to break the awkward silence.

"Really?" Trev said.

And, to my surprise, he stood there at the end of his driveway while I told him how Uncle Vic's house had been burned to smithereens. I exaggerated the damage and hammed up the image of Uncle Vic in his tighty-whities until Trev started to smile.

"Now I have a *bunkmate*," I said, exaggerating the word so I sounded more like a gangster sharing a jail cell than a kid sharing his room with his uncle.

Trev laughed.

"So, anyway, that's how I ended up choosing firefighting as my career. It was a total accident."

We laughed together, and before I knew it, Trev was filling me in on what I'd missed in class — which was a lot. We had to do a report and interviews for class and a presentation board for our community career day. And we only had till the end of the month to do it.

"I thought Career and Tech was supposed to be easy," I groaned. "That's why I chose it as my option."

"It's a split class of seventh and eighth graders. You should've known it would be tough."

I winced. Trev was right — as usual. He may be younger than me, but that didn't stop him from being a whole lot smarter. "So why did you take it?" I asked. "Not getting enough of a challenge in the dojo?"

Trev's freckles blended together as he scrunched up his face. "Like you care," he grumbled.

My reference to martial arts, an attempt to bridge the gap between us, had obviously backfired. I tried to change the subject. "Do you want to work on —"

Trev cut me off with a shake of his head. "Later, Hudson."

"Fine." I ran the toe of my high-top across the leaf-clogged gutter as Trev disappeared into his house without looking back. I knew his gran would be waiting inside with some yummy homemade snack — ice cream and applesauce or jam-filled sandwich cookies (or both) — while his parents stayed out, working late into the night at the hardware store they owned in town.

Trev was still pissed off at me, and I still didn't know how to fix it.

It was true that I'd been a jerk. But I'd already apologized a million times — even before the start of junior high.

Trev hadn't just sent me to the penalty box; he'd thrown me out of the league.

CHAPTER THREE

I spent the rest of the afternoon shooting hoops, hoping Trev might be tempted to come out for some one-on-one. But no. With each basket, I got madder and madder, until I finally gave up and went inside.

When Mom came home, I stayed in my room. I was still fuming over Aidan, Matthew, Liam ... and Trev. As I doodled on the corner of my homework book, I could hear her talking to Uncle Vic in the kitchen.

After a while, curiosity and hunger (my afternoon snack, three fluffernutter sandwiches and a glass of chocolate milk, was a distant memory) got the better of me. I went prowling downstairs.

"Hey, Mom, what's for dinner?" I sat on my stool at the kitchen counter, hoping for some takeout. Chinese would be good. Then I noticed Uncle Vic was wearing an apron. Great.

Mom nudged me off the stool.

"We're in the dining room tonight, Hudson."

"Why?" I asked, ignoring the fact that there were only two stools at the counter.

She ignored me right back.

I watched Uncle Vic carry a big wooden bowl from the kitchen to the dining room, which was less than four feet away and about the size of a goalie crease. "Hey, kid. Ready to chow down?"

"Hey, Uncle Vic." I followed him to the table and dropped heavily into the spot that had obviously been set for me — with a plastic cup instead of glass. I surveyed the meal, laid out in serving dishes in the center of the small, round table. No meat. No potatoes. Just salads. "Is this all we're having? Rabbit food?"

"Don't be rude." Mom ruffled my hair and then sat down beside me. "As long as Uncle Vic makes dinner, we'll eat what he eats."

I ran my hand through the thick brown hair that had grown out of my brush cut. It was finally long enough that it didn't stand on end, adding more unwanted inches to my height. "But athletes need protein."

"I don't think you need to worry, kid." Uncle Vic dumped salad and half a jar of dressing onto his plate. "Looks to me like you grew another foot while I was on tour."

I slouched down low in my chair, wondering whether his milk run through Pennsylvania qualified as a tour. "I'm not worried about getting taller," I said through clenched teeth. "I'm worried about muscle mass."

Mom smiled sympathetically. "Just be glad your uncle is no longer a freegan."

Uncle Vic laughed. "Those were some crazy times."

"Crazy?" Mom made a face like she'd just caught a whiff of my sweaty hockey gloves. "Try disgusting."

I nodded in agreement. I couldn't imagine eating food from a garbage bin. But Uncle Vic had insisted that grocery stores and restaurants threw away tons of perfectly good food every day. For months, he'd saved the world — and money — with what he called his anticonsumerism lifestyle. Then he'd ended up in the hospital with stomach problems.

"You can get lots of protein from a healthy, vegetarian diet," Uncle Vic said, holding up a forkful of chickpeas and sunflower seeds to demonstrate.

"Maybe enough for musicians," I said as I buttered another thick piece of multigrain bread, "but not enough for athletes."

"What about Georges Laraque from the Montreal Canadiens? He's vegan."

"He's also retired," I muttered, even though I'd

heard rumors that he was making a comeback in Norway or something.

"There's Mike Zigomanis." Uncle Vic shoveled lettuce into his mouth. "He played a few games for the Penguins," he added, as if it were possible there was an NHL player I didn't know.

"I don't play hockey anymore."

"What?" Uncle Vic raised his eyebrows, wrinkling his otherwise smooth and shiny forehead. "Since when?"

"Since summer."

"Isn't hockey a winter sport?"

"You try out for the next season as soon as playoffs are over in the spring," Mom said quietly, "so you can make a decision about summer training."

Uncle Vic's fingers drummed the table next to his empty plate. "How come no one told me?"

"Hudson doesn't like to talk about it," Mom said.

I stood up so fast that I banged my knee against the table. Grabbing my plate, I hobbled into the kitchen and scraped the rest of my salad into the garburator. Over the running water, I could hear Mom tell Uncle Vic how I'd been cut from my AAA team. That I'd hung up my skates because I didn't want to drop down a level.

The sharp pain in my knee was overpowered by

a familiar ache — the feeling of being battered and bruised on the inside — as I thought about what my coach had said: "You grew too quickly, Hudson. I thought some bulk would help you, but it's slowed you down. And your height has really affected your stick handling. I'm sorry, sport, but it happens."

His words had crushed me. Hockey had been my life. It was still my favorite sport in the world, but now I was a spectator instead of a star. Mom had encouraged me to keep going, convinced that I'd get the coordination back, and then my height would be an advantage. But I didn't want to.

Here's what I knew: Mom had lied. She'd always told me that I could have whatever I wanted if I tried hard enough. That I could be whatever I wanted to be.

But that wasn't true. I'd tried and failed. There was nothing I could do. No one could control how much they grew. Or when.

Not even Mom.

***

When the dishes were done (to my standards, not Mom's), I went back to the dining room to ask Uncle Vic for the firefighter's business card.

"It's all that time you spend in bars and restaurants,"

Mom was saying. "Those places are full of smoke and — "

Uncle Vic cut her off. "When's the last time you were in a bar, Martha? There's been a smoking ban in New York State for over ten years. None of the big cities allow you to light up anywhere near — "

"You don't have a healthy lifestyle." Mom leaned forward and pointed her finger at him. "You refuse to grow up, and now you're suffering the consequences."

"Don't get all high-and-mighty on me, sis." Uncle Vic's voice was getting louder. "It's just some smoke from last night. Don't make such a big deal about it."

I could see the cracks in Mom's usual mask of calm and control: red eyes that matched her face, a twitch at the side of her mouth. She didn't lose it often, but when she did, look out. "Don't make a big deal of it? How does someone sleep through a kettle whistle, a smoke alarm and a frantic neighbor trying to bust down the door?"

"Dunno, sis." Uncle Vic looked tired and defeated. Even his hair hung limp and straight, instead of messy and fun like it usually was. "Being on the road must've really worn me out ..."

"That feeble excuse is not going to cut it. Do you

know how long I spent on the phone with the fire department?" Mom's hands were flying, her pointed finger stabbing the air as she spoke. "When are you going to grow up? No insurance. A suspicious fire. Arson investigators calling me at work —"

"The fire's suspicious?" I interrupted.

Mom and Uncle Vic looked up, surprise showing on each of their faces in totally opposite ways: Mom's lips pursed together tighter than the stitching on a goalie pad, Uncle Vic's mouth hanging open. They'd been so deep in conversation that neither of them had noticed me standing there.

"That's wh—" A barking cough overtook Uncle Vic and stopped him from talking.

"Never mind, Hudson." Mom pointed at Uncle Vic again. "You are having that X-ray tomorrow."

When he'd finished hacking up his lung, Uncle Vic turned to me instead of Mom. "I hear you're going out for the basketball team."

I frowned. Mom must have included that detail in her account of my hockey disaster, determined, as always, to put a happily-ever-after spin on everything.

"Tryouts are tomorrow," I mumbled.

"Excited?"

"Nervous."

"A superathlete like you?" Uncle Vic stroked his goatee. "What do you have to be nervous about?"

I shrugged. Basketball had been Mom's idea. She'd enrolled me in summer camp to get my mind off hockey (and keep tabs on me while she worked). As much as I'd wanted to hate it — preferring to wallow in my hockey-fueled depression — I'd been hooked by a breakaway on my very first day. I loved the feel of the ball on my palm almost as much as the feel of the puck on my stick. And when the ball swooshed through the net? Well, that was the best.

I didn't want to try out for the school team — I had to. At the same time, the thought of failing again tugged at my stomach like food poisoning. I didn't know if I could handle not making the team. Again.

"Basketball should be a slam dunk for you. Check it out — you're like Shaquille O'Neal. Only younger, lighter and whiter." Uncle Vic laughed at his joke.

He was the only one.

Uncle Vic stood up and stretched. "Well, good luck tomorrow, kid. Break a leg, as they say in show biz."

"I hope not," I said, trying to keep the attitude out of my voice. And failing.

"It's just an expression," said Uncle Vic.

"I know."

Mom brushed crumbs off the table into her palm. "Why don't you two go out and shoot some hoops while I finish cleaning up?"

"Sorry." Uncle Vic yawned. "Too tired."

Mom bit her lip and tilted her head inquisitively. "Again with the fatigue. Is this common?"

"Cut me some slack, sis. I'm just a little sleepy. Next time, kid."

"No problem," I said, covering my disappointment with a wave of my hand.

"Okay, then I'm turning in. See you in the morning." Uncle Vic headed upstairs toward my room — our room.

I flopped down on the sofa and clicked on the TV, pushing the On button much harder than necessary. The more I thought about it, the more Uncle Vic's behavior seemed strange. How many thirty-three-year-olds went to bed before seven o'clock? Was he up to something? Whatever it was, I hoped it wouldn't involve hogging my bedroom the entire time he stayed with us.

Mom came into the living room a couple minutes (and a hundred channels) later. "I'm sure you'll be great at tryouts tomorrow, Hudson."

"Whatever," I mumbled, pretending to be interested in a commercial for some new energy drink.

Mom reached over the back of our worn leather sofa — the one she'd rushed out to buy as soon as I'd been diagnosed with asthma — and put both hands on my shoulders. "Remember to bring your inhaler."

"Don't need it," I said without taking my eyes off the TV.

"Just in case."

"*It appears that you're asymptomatic,*" I said in a high-pitched voice, mimicking Dr. M., the respirologist who'd followed me since I was diagnosed at four. I could do a pretty mean imitation, thanks to all the time I'd spent with her over the years. But I wouldn't see her again. "I've outgrown it."

"She warned us of a relapse." Mom gently massaged my neck with her thumb. "You've already had two colds, and cold-and-flu season has only just begun."

I swiveled around to face her. "I've outgrown it," I said again. As if repeating a statement could make it true.

"Your spirometry result was good, but ..." Mom gave me a you-know-what-I-mean look, then she picked up one of the many clean dust cloths she keeps stashed around the house.

"Whatever," I said, crossing my arms over my chest and turning back to the TV.

"Bring your inhaler to the tryout, Hudson," Mom said firmly as she started dusting. "Don't forget."

"Fine. I won't."

But I did.

CHAPTER FOUR

"Awesome job, everyone," Coach Koniuk yelled. The sound of sneakers squeaking against the polished gym floor stopped abruptly. "Now grab your water bottles and gather 'round."

I walked over to the bench and tried to catch my breath. The tryout had started with fifteen suicide sprints. The most we'd ever done at summer camp was ten. This was going to be some test.

"First, I want to thank you all for coming," Coach Koniuk said, rubbing his hands together. "It's great to see so many of you trying out for the team."

I pushed myself into the circle surrounding the coach, intentionally bumping my shoulder against Trev's. What was he doing here? He hadn't shown much interest in basketball since I'd raised the net on my driveway to full height.

I tried to shake off the nervous energy buzzing through me as I examined the crowd. There were more wannabe basketball players than I'd expected (or wanted). Our school was in hockey country; any sport that used a ball instead of a puck was considered second-rate at best.

"It's going to be hard for us to get gym time until volleyball season ends in December," Coach Koniuk continued, "so Coach Johansen and I are going to hold tryouts for the junior and senior teams together. And for some practices, the girls' teams will be joining us."

There was a collective groan, and I felt Trev tense up beside me.

"Relax, boys," Coach Koniuk said, "girls don't bite."

"But they do wiggle." Aidan rotated his hips like a hula dancer, then held his hands up to his chest to mimic a bikini top. "And jiggle."

There were a couple of scoffs and a snort of appreciation from some of the other guys.

"Enough!" Coach Koniuk bellowed. "If you want to be part of this team, you're going to have to show some respect."

Aidan spread his arms out wide, exaggerating the movement of his hands away from his chest. "I meant *dribble*, Coach."

Coach Koniuk ignored him. "Tryouts will last all month. I've posted the schedule on the board. The teams will be announced at the end of October. That should give us plenty of time to practice before the season begins in January. Any questions?"

"How many will you pick for each team?" I asked.

"Ten to twelve players per team, depending on how things go," Coach Koniuk answered.

I did the math. Half of us would be cut — mostly seventh graders, assuming that the junior team would have a lot of eighth graders. The senior team would probably have some star eighth graders, but mostly ninth graders.

Coach Koniuk looked around. "Anyone else?"

"Will there be any drug testing?" Aidan smirked, looking straight at me. "It seems possible some of us might be abusing growth hormones or something. With all due respect to those of us who favor clean competition ..."

Nervous laughter filled the gym. My stomach clenched.

Coach Koniuk gave Aidan a warning look, then ignored him. He clapped his hands. "I'm going to divide you up for drills. We're going to start with crosscourt sprint and shoot."

The seventh graders went with Coach Johansen. The eighth and ninth graders went with Coach Koniuk.

We spent the next hour learning the crosscourt-sprint-and-shoot drill, which was a sequence of passing, sprinting, jump shots and free throws. We took turns, so I had lots of time to check out the competition.

Here's what I knew: I was the tallest seventh grader but not the fastest. And my shooting percentage was better than most but not the best.

Next we did some dribbling drills, including the two-ball dribble and full-court zigzags. I was feeling pretty beat-up by the time we got to play some three-on-three. My chest felt tight, and I was starting to wheeze, but I could see the coaches were taking notes, so I gave it my all. Practice had to be over soon.

I had just finished picking up a rebound and was about to turn and shoot when Coach Koniuk blew the whistle. "We're going to end practice with ten suicide sprints. Go!"

I made what I hoped was a quick, crisp pass to Coach Johansen and ran for the baseline. Without stopping, I sprinted to the closest free-throw line. Back to the baseline. To half-court. Baseline. Far free-throw line. Baseline. Endline.

I started to cough as I ran across the court back to baseline again. I kept running. Far free-throw line. Baseline. Half-court.

The lines were starting to look fuzzy. I stopped running, but I couldn't catch my breath.

"You okay, Hudson?" Trev was standing next to me.

"Fine," I gasped as I pounded on my chest. "Keep going."

Trev followed me as I sprinted toward the free-throw line. "Where's your puffer?"

I didn't answer. I couldn't.

Where was baseline?

I stopped and crouched over, feeling like I'd swallowed one of the balls. I couldn't get any air into my lungs, no matter how hard I tried. Frantically, I gulped and gasped, as if I were trapped under a sheet of ice in a frozen lake.

"Coach!" yelled Trev. "Hudson is having an asthma attack!"

I'm not entirely sure what happened next. I heard Trev tell me to calm down. I felt Coach Koniuk and Coach Johansen lead me out of the gym to the nurse's office. My arms hung limp over their shoulders.

Someone handed me an inhaler. "Can you do it?"

I shook it, removed the cap with my teeth, spit it out and put the mouthpiece between my lips. I pressed down on the canister and breathed in as much as I could. Then I did it again.

Within a few minutes, I felt better. Like there was only one elephant sitting on my chest instead of a hundred.

"Do we need to call an ambulance?" Coach Koniuk asked the school nurse, who was standing next to him.

"I'm okay," I answered for her.

"I've already called your mom," the nurse said. "Good thing you have an asthma care plan."

I sat on my hands to stop them from shaking. "My mom works at the hospital."

"She should be here soon, then." Coach Koniuk put his hand on my shoulder and spoke to Trev. "What's your name again?"

"Trevor Bach."

"You okay to stay with him till his mom comes?"

"Yes."

"Great. Take care of yourself, Hudson, and I'll see you two at practice on Friday."

I nodded. "Sure thing, Coach."

Trev didn't say anything.

"If you need me, I'll be right there." The nurse pointed at a desk behind the glass partition dividing the room. "I have to write an incident report."

"Well, at least Coach Koniuk knows our names now," I said when she was gone.

Trev's legs bounced impatiently in the chair next to mine. "Not cool, Hudson."

I shut the door on this thought — that I'd made a bad first impression on the coach — and decided to focus on Trev instead. "You're into basketball now?"

Trev shook his head. "Gran's making me try out. She says I need to focus on 'regular American sports' now that I have my black belt in karate."

"But you'd rather do judo," I guessed. "Or jujitsu."

Trev shook his head. "I want to achieve the next *dan* level in karate," he said. "*Ni dan.*"

"You mean you can do better than a black belt?"

"There are ten degrees or *dan* levels." He spoke like he was giving a prepared speech. "I'm a *sho dan* black belt, the first degree. I want to get to second degree, so I can be an instructor, but Gran says it's a waste of time. She wants me to focus on my religious studies and making friends at school."

"That sucks."

"Yeah, well, trying out is no big deal. And when I get cut" — Trev snapped two fingers together like scissors — "I'll go back to doing what I want to do."

I shuddered at the word *cut* — the sports equivalent of a fail. An epic fail. A humiliating fail. Not just one of those red Fs that appear on the top of a graded paper. Being cut from a sports team was a public fail, something everyone knew about, something that could change the course of your life. There was no way to hide it — kind of like an asthma attack.

I thought about how much getting cut from hockey had changed my life. It could not happen again. I needed sports and I needed friends. Come to think of it, so did Trev. Maybe being on the team would stop the bullying. Aidan wouldn't pick on him if they were teammates, would he?

"What makes you so sure you'll get cut?" I asked.

"I'm too short for basketball."

"It's not all about height," I said, even though Mom had chosen basketball as my replacement sport for exactly that reason. "Steve Nash is only six foot three, and he's one of the best point guards to ever play the game."

Trev lifted my inhaler off the nurse's table and held it up between us, dangling it from his fingers like it was a dirty jockstrap. "Maybe it's not the right sport for you either."

I grabbed it out of his hand. "Asthma never stopped me from playing hockey."

"What triggered the attack, then?"

"It wasn't an attack," I said, refusing to believe

that my asthma wasn't completely gone. "Just a bit of reactivity. No big deal."

Trev frowned. "Why didn't you bring your inhaler?"

"I just forgot," I said. "There's a lot going on at my house. I'm tired."

"Because of Uncle Vic?"

"I guess." I crossed my arms over my chest, wishing I could say that Uncle Vic and I had been up all night watching sports. Or that he'd taken me to the bar to watch his band play.

I wasn't about to tell Trev that my rock-star uncle had gone to bed way earlier than me — and had snored so loudly that I could hear it right through my headphones. I'd tried everything to make it stop, but even hitting him with a pillow and snapping in his ear hadn't worked. Waking Uncle Vic was like mission impossible.

Still, I wished that the nurse had called him instead of Mom. I was sure Trev's complaining would be nothing compared to the lecture I was about to get from her.

But I was wrong.

When she finally arrived, all she said was, "Let's go."

CHAPTER FIVE

As we followed Mom out of the nurse's office and past the gym, the empty hallway seemed creepy and unfamiliar.

"You missed the changeroom," I said.

Mom blazed ahead of us at roughly the speed of light. "No time," she said over her shoulder.

"But we're still in our gym clothes."

"I'm parked close to the door. You won't freeze."

"Can we give Trev a lift?"

"Of course." Mom's pace slowed to the speed of sound. "Thank you for helping Hudson, Trevor. It's good to see you two together again. We'll drop you off on our way to the hospital."

The hospital? "But I'm fine, Mom! It was just a little reaction. I only needed a small puff."

She didn't say anything else until we were all in the car. "If you're going to make a habit of forgetting your inhaler, you're going to have to go back to taking Flovent."

"But Mom —"

"And wearing your medical ID bracelet."

I groaned. "But —"

"I'll make an appointment with Dr. M. to discuss it. Right now, I have to get back to Mercy General to pick up your uncle."

"He's at the hospital?"

Mom peeled out of the parking lot. "He's been there all day," she said.

.·.

When we got to the hospital, Mom headed directly to the ER. It was clear from the way she marched through the halls that she'd worked there for a million years. We passed the cardiology waiting area, where I used to play when Mom couldn't get childcare. From there, I knew how to follow the lines painted on the floor to get to the pediatric intensive care unit. Before I outgrew my asthma, I'd wound up there a couple of times.

The rest of the place was a mystery to me, even though my mom spent most of her days there, looking at people's hearts. She used to do ultrasounds for pregnant women, but that was a long time ago, before we'd lost my baby brother. Not that I remembered anything about it — I was only two when Darwyn died.

We entered the ER through a back door labeled *Staff Only*. Uncle Vic was sitting on a stretcher wearing a hospital gown the color of green vomit. I flashed back to the image of him sitting in the ambulance in his underwear, wrapped in a blanket, on the night of the fire. It was freakishly similar, except the audience was even bigger this time. The blue privacy curtain had been pushed to the side, and a gang of health-care workers hovered around him.

"Martha, you're back." A man in blue scrubs held a medical chart in one hand and reading glasses in the other. He was not smiling, but Uncle Vic was (at one of the nurses).

"Sorry, I had to step out, Dr. Carreira." Mom's bloodshot eyes flashed angrily in my direction. "Do you have any updates?"

"I've ordered a complete pulmonary function test. It will be performed in conjunction with a referral to the respiratory and neurodiagnostic clinic in Buffalo."

"The spirometry results are that bad?" asked Mom.

"They're suggestive of chronic obstructive pulmonary disease."

"COPD? But he's only in his thirties —"

The doctor cut her off with a click of his pen. "I know. He's too young. That's why we need further investigation: X-rays, arterial blood gas ..." The doctor spoke like a sports announcer doing a play-by-play.

I didn't understand anything the doctor (or my mom) was saying, so I stopped listening and stared at the machine attached to Uncle Vic's finger. There was a wavy blue line on the monitor with numbers next to it that kept changing from ninety to ninety-two. I stood there imagining I was watching the scoreboard at an NBA game.

"Hey, kid." Uncle Vic tapped me on the arm to get my attention. "I heard you made a scene at practice."

"It was nothing," I said quietly so I wouldn't interrupt the doctor. I hoped the more Mom concentrated on Uncle Vic's health problems, the less she'd think about mine. And the sooner we would be out of there. The Sabres game was starting soon.

"You and me are just the same," Uncle Vic said with a grin. "Not going to let a few lung problems slow us down."

The nurse next to Uncle Vic turned to look at me. "You have lung problems?"

The doctor must have heard the question because he stopped midsentence and finally looked my way. "And you are?"

"Hudson."

"My son," added Mom.

The doctor narrowed his eyes, examining me like I was a skeleton hanging out in the corner of a lecture theater. "He looks too old to be your son."

Mom blushed. "I did have him when I was young ..."

"No, really," the doctor said, still looking at me. "And his features are different —"

"He's my nephew," Uncle Vic interrupted. "Tall for his age."

"Okay, then." The doctor hooked his reading glasses over his ears and scribbled something in Uncle Vic's chart. "I think I'd better get some family history."

"There's not much to know, Dr. Carreira," Mom said quickly. "It's just me and Hudson, and he's healthy apart from childhood asthma."

"Which I've outgrown," I added for Mom's benefit more than the doctor's.

"Any history of lung disease on his father's side of the family?"

Mom's face scrunched up as if on reflex.

"Hudson's father lives on the coast," said Uncle

Vic. "There's no contact. He could be dead for all we know."

A layer of stale hospital air, too thick to breathe, closed in on me. No one talked about my dad — ever. There were no pictures, no mementos. Nothing. And yet suddenly I'd been forced to think about him, or at least the idea of him, twice in just a few days. I inhaled slowly, trying to focus on the here and now like my hockey coach had told us to do. I shoved the thought of my dad to the back of my brain, where it belonged.

Dr. Carreira broke the trance that had come over us at the mention of my dad and death. "Ethnicity?"

"European. Hudson's father's Croatian," Mom said softly.

I took a sharp breath. Croatian was a lot less shocking than dead. Still, it was the most I'd ever heard Mom say about him.

"Our roots are mainly English," added Mom, "mixed with a little bit of Dutch and ..."

As she rattled on like she was listing recipe ingredients, the doctor stared at me as if we'd both been cast in an episode of *Grey's Anatomy*. "Ethnic diversity is good from a genetic point of view," he said. "Do you have any children, Victor?"

"None that I know of," Uncle Vic answered with a chuckle.

The doctor scribbled something on the medical chart. "Do you have any other brothers or sisters?"

"Just Martha," Uncle Vic replied.

"Any half sibs?"

"No," said Mom.

"Any health problems for you, Martha?"

"No."

The doctor pushed on the end of the pen so the ballpoint went in and out, in and out. The clicking noise — among other things — was starting to annoy me. "Victor, I think you need to see a genetic counselor."

A look of horror crossed Mom's face. "But we just told you — there is no family history."

"I think there's one associated with the respiratory and neurodiagnostic clinic. I'll add a note to the referral," announced Dr. Carreira.

"Don't you think we're overreacting?" Mom nibbled at her thumbnail. "Should we maybe just repeat the spirometry test to rule out lung disease?"

"I'm not ruling out anything without further testing," said the doctor. "This could be COPD. It could be the synergistic effect of an upper respiratory infection, smoke and medication. It could be part of a genetic syndrome. It could be nothing."

"It's nothing." Uncle Vic scratched at his neck, and the green hospital gown shifted, exposing the tree tattoo that covered his shoulders and back. I studied the nurse's face for a reaction to the dark lines that snaked their way down his body, forming the roots of the tree. Every time I saw them, I shuddered at the thought of a needle injecting ink into his skin — a process Mom had described to me in excruciating detail. More than once.

The nurse didn't even flinch. She'd obviously seen things a lot more shocking. But Mom still looked horrified as she clutched her bony wrist — her own flawless skin so pale that it almost glowed in the dark.

Uncle Vic didn't bother to adjust his gown as he swung his legs off the stretcher. "Are we done here?"

"Just one more quick blood test," the doctor said, making large checks in small boxes on a page attached to the front of the chart.

Uncle Vic stuck out his arm and turned on the charm. "I'm starting to feel like a pincushion," he said to the nurse. "Can you get me some type of prescription for the pain?"

How could a couple blood tests hurt someone with a tattoo as big as Uncle Vic's? As the nurse prodded his arm for a vein, I excused myself. I hoped they were showing the game on the TV in the waiting room.

Walking away from the tiny curtained space, I could hear Mom and Dr. Carreira exchanging medical jargon in low tones. Uncle Vic was singing to the nurse — either to distract himself from the needle or to score some real sympathy. As corny as it was, I didn't doubt that the nurse would be into it. Women always seemed to like Uncle Vic. At least at first. I'd never known him to have any long-term relationships, just an ongoing stream of good-looking girlfriends.

Of course, that didn't mean he'd never had anyone special in his life. Anything was possible, and I was starting to think there was a lot I didn't know about my quirky little family.

CHAPTER SIX

Things at home went back to their regular, boring routine for the rest of the week. Even Uncle Vic's healthy, veggie dinners started to seem normal.

Sometimes I liked having him around. He made a mess and upset some of Mom's heavily guarded routine. But the rest of the time, he was just there, complaining about how much he missed his guitar, even though Mom had pulled an old one out of the closet for him. (I'd yet to get a straight answer on where, or *who*, it had come from.)

Anyway, our boring home was still boring, but somehow Uncle Vic made it more tolerable.

School was a different story. The work was much harder in junior high, and I was already falling behind. One of my teachers sent a note home with a request that I redo my completed homework sheet, which was now covered in red ink. Mom blamed it on my lack of privacy and cleared some space in the basement for Uncle Vic. But I still couldn't sleep through the night, even without Uncle Vic's snoring. It was like the back of my brain was getting too full — the thoughts I kept locked up there were constantly trying to escape.

By Friday I hadn't even started my report for Career & Tech. So I was totally unprepared when Ms. Lavender asked us to interview each other. We were supposed to act as if we already worked in our chosen professions. Even worse, she paired me with Willow — the last person I wanted to catch me unprepared.

"I heard you had an asthma attack at basketball practice," she said after we'd turned our desks so we faced each other.

I nodded, feeling defensive and exposed, like I'd been sent to the box for a penalty I didn't deserve. How far had the story spread?

Willow stared at me, uncomfortable, like she expected me to start hacking up snot all over her like I had in preschool. "I almost didn't recognize you," she said.

I clenched my teeth in anticipation of some crack about my height — the kind of comment I should be used to by now, but wasn't. Growing tall enough to be mistaken for your mom's boyfriend was humiliating enough. But I still didn't have a good comeback for all those references to the Jolly Green Giant, Big Foot, Paul Bunyan and, of course, Big Bird.

But Willow didn't mention my height. Instead, she hit an even sorer spot. "Haven't really seen you since you got held back."

I sank into my hard chair, my face flush with embarrassment. I'd missed a lot of school in second grade because of my asthma. Willow wasn't ahead of me because she was supersmart. I was behind her because I was superdumb. With a pain-in-the-butt illness. "Yeah."

Willow smiled mischievously. "*Qué bueno verte de nuevo.*"

"You still speak Spanish?" I asked, remembering the flash cards she'd plastered all over her room — a desperate attempt to teach me her native language so I could play the part of a Mexican prince at her tea parties. Which I'd only attended extremely reluctantly. To say it hadn't worked would be a mammoth understatement. Anyone who grew up watching *Dora the Explorer* knew more Spanish than me, no matter how hard Willow tried.

Now she rolled her eyes like I'd just said something really stupid — which I had, of course.

"I speak Portuguese and French now, too," she said.

"Then why do you want to be a postal worker?"

I asked. "Why not a translator for the United Nations or something?"

"Why do you want to be a firefighter?"

"I don't know," I said.

Willow laughed. "I guess you're not ready to do the interview, then."

"Uh. Not exactly. Sorry."

"That's okay." Willow tucked her long black hair behind her ears. Immediately, one of her curls bounced back in defiance. Willow ignored it, but I could not. "I'll go first," she said.

"Thanks." I watched the curl out of the corner of my eye.

Willow sorted through the papers on her desk. "That means you have to ask the questions."

"Uh, yeah, of course. So ... why do you want to be a postal worker?"

Willow laughed again, and it sounded kind of nice. Her voice was high-pitched and airy but not too girly or squealish. "For this assignment, you're supposed to pretend I'm already a postal worker."

"Right, sorry," I stammered. "Why did you become a postal worker?"

"Because I wanted to spend every day outdoors," said Willow. "And I like being active."

"Active? Don't you just walk up and down the street delivering mail?"

Willow frowned. "Walking is healthy. And you have to carry a heavy bag."

"Right. Of course," I said, even though it didn't exactly sound like a workout. "Sorry."

"I just mean that I didn't want to be stuck behind a desk all day."

Willow seemed so sure of herself, like Trev did when he talked about karate or gaming.

Not being behind a desk sounded good to me, too. I realized something: "That's the same with firefighting."

"Plus, mail carriers set their own schedules." Willow talked with her hands, like Mom did when she was giving me a lecture. "They have a route. They deliver the mail. When the mail is delivered, their workday is done. There's no standing around wondering what to do. When you're busy, you're busy. When you're not, you're not."

"Same with firefighting," I blurted out. I wasn't buying Willow's sales job on mail delivery, but she was starting to make me think that firefighting was actually kind of cool. More than a profession glorified by the imagination of a kindergarten kid, anyway.

Willow scratched her chin — she had a dimple there that I'd never noticed before. "Not really. Firefighters sit around the fire station for hours at a time, waiting for a call, and when they finally get one, they have to instantly spring to action." Willow twirled her hand in the air above her head. "That sounds totally different to me."

"Yeah, but when they're hanging out at the fire station, they can do what they want: eat, play games, work out ..."

Willow creased her eyebrows together. "We're supposed to be talking about me —"

"And firefighters get to compete in the World Police and Fire Games," I said, suddenly remembering all the reasons I'd wanted to be a firefighter when I was little.

"So you really do want to be a firefighter?" Willow leaned forward in her chair. "I got the feeling you were just blowing off the assignment."

"Firefighting's awesome. And the World Police and Fire Games are almost as big as the Olympics," I said, even though I didn't think it was true.

"I like sports, too," said Willow, "but probably not as much as you do."

"Weren't you thinking of being a sports broadcaster?"

Willow shrugged. "Well, I like mail more."

"But mail is so ... lame," I said, unable to stop the thought from tumbling out.

Willow's jaw stiffened. "My dad works for the US Postal Service."

"Oh." I wanted to crawl under my desk, though there was no way I would fit. I'd forgotten her dad was a mail carrier, our mail carrier, in fact. Or he had been until he was promoted to postmaster of Bluster's central post office.

But Willow didn't look too offended. "What does your dad do?" she asked.

I pulled back from my desk like I'd been burned. Another reference to my dad. From Willow of all people. How could she forget? "I don't have a dad."

"Of course you do —"

I cut her off before she had a chance to lecture me on the birds and the bees. "Yeah, but he's just, uh ..." My voice cracked. "Gone."

Willow must have sensed my embarrassment, which, given my red-hot face and stammered speech, didn't exactly require psychic ability. Her voice softened: "I knew you didn't live with your dad, but I assumed he was still around."

I cleared my throat and concentrated on keeping my voice even. "No," I said. "He's not."

"No birthday cards? Christmas phone calls? Video chats? Nothing?"

"Nothing."

"Oh." Willow bit her lip. "I'm sorry."

"It's no big deal." I tried to sound casual as my

heart hammered in my chest like it was competing for a world record. "But we're way off topic."

Willow pushed her hair off her forehead. "Right. Ask me another question. A good one."

I didn't come up with anything that could be described as good. But somehow I managed to cover the basics, like what kind of training you need to deliver the mail. Willow answered all my questions patiently, even though I made a few more stupid comments before the class was over.

"You're lucky we have guest speakers next week. But you'd better be ready for my questions next time," Willow joked when the bell rang.

As we stood to turn our desks, she caught my gaze and didn't let go. Standing there eye to eye, I realized she was almost the same height as me. I felt like I was standing at center court, ready to take the tip-off against someone superhard to beat.

"I will be," I said, even though I'd forgotten what I needed to be ready for.

"Firefighting's a pretty decent profession," Willow said as she gathered her books together. "I can totally see you doing it."

A grin pulled at the corners of my mouth as I lowered my head, stepped into the aisle and rammed right into Trev.

"Whoa!" he shouted.

"Sorry," I said, reaching out to steady him. "Ready for practice?"

"Yeah." Trev shook my arm off his shoulder. "So?"

"Let's head to the gym together." I made the suggestion for his benefit as well as mine. Safety in numbers and all that. Bullies were less likely to pick on a pair of kids, even if one hated the other. Trev had to see that, right?

But his face soured, and I knew he was about to blow me off.

Then suddenly his expression changed. "Hey, Willow," he said.

I hadn't realized she was still there.

"Hey, Trev," Willow said. "How are things at the Roundhouse?"

"Deadlier than ever." Trev smiled.

"How do you know about the Roundhouse?" I asked.

"I took some karate lessons there," Willow said.

Trev grabbed her backpack off the floor and handed it to her. "Haven't seen you in the dojo lately."

"It was just a summer thing." Willow flipped the backpack over her shoulder. Her hair followed in a cascade of curls that smelled like shampoo.

My gut knotted. I took a step toward the door. "You coming with?" I asked Trev.

"Wait up for me, you guys," Willow said as Trev started to push ahead of me.

"What for?" I demanded, not meaning to be rude. It's just that Willow had flustered me enough for one day, and I needed this practice to be perfect. Or at least a heck of a lot better than the last one.

"I'll walk with you," said Willow. "The girls are practicing, too."

"Oh," Trev and I said at the same time.

"Don't sound so excited." Willow chuckled. She didn't notice Aidan strutting up the aisle behind her until he was close enough to poke her in the ribs. She jumped. "Oh! Aidan! You scared me!"

"So, you're playing basketball with the big boys tonight, eh, Willow?" Aidan flashed us all a lopsided smile. "Maybe you can teach Wheezy here a few moves."

Willow frowned. "His name is Hudson."

"I think Wheezy suits him. It's better than Big Bird," Aidan said, "even if he is too tall to hang out with the seven dwarves."

"Let's go," said Trev as he trudged toward the door.

"Right behind you, Elmo," Aidan said. "I hope today's practice is as exciting as the last one."

I reached into the pocket of my hoodie and gripped my inhaler. Then I visualized myself boxing out

Aidan for every rebound. "I'll show you exciting," I muttered under my breath.

❥❥❥

Practice started with drills, of course. But this time, Coach Koniuk didn't divide us up by grade — he divided us by height. And we didn't just share the gym with the girls, we played with them.

That's how I ended up paired off with Willow — again. This time for some two-on-two against Aidan, whose partner was a ninth-grade girl who'd started for the senior team last year. I thought we were going to get creamed.

But I was wrong.

The game was decided by two points.

Aidan took a jump shot that bounced off the backboard and rolled around the rim of the net but didn't drop. I stepped in front of him while he was still admiring his shot and grabbed the rebound before it had a chance to fall. I passed to Willow at the point. Without hesitating, she squared up to the net and let the ball fly, following through with a perfect flick of the wrist. She scored just as Coach Koniuk blew the whistle to end the practice.

Nothing but net — sweetest shot I've ever seen.

CHAPTER SEVEN

On Saturday, Uncle Vic had an appointment with E. O. Bouchier from the fire department. I begged to go with him. I hadn't started my Career & Tech project yet, and I needed some information to avoid looking stupid in front of Willow. Not that she was my only motivation. The grade I'd gotten on my last math test was the real kicker. I couldn't afford to fall behind in any of my other classes. Plus, I was kind of pumped about the whole firefighting thing.

Uncle Vic didn't take much convincing — taking me helped him wangle a deal to borrow Mom's car.

When we arrived at the station, he introduced me as "the tagalong" and explained why I was with him. E. O. Bouchier took it from there, giving me more information than I could ever cram into my overstuffed brain. I should've brought a recorder or, at least, a pen and paper so I could jot down some notes.

Turns out there's a lot more to being a firefighter than most people know. They don't just sit around eating spaghetti dinners at the fire station, waiting for the bell to ring so they can slide down a pole, take a ride in a big truck and save a kitten from a tree.

For starters, there are many different kinds of firefighters. E. O. (he hates being called Mr. Bouchier) started out working for the National Wildlife Refuge as a fire specialist, which means he was paid to start forest fires and put them out. He even got to ride in helicopters with smoke jumpers, who parachute into remote areas to fight wildfires. He stopped all that "dangerous stuff" when he got married and became a dad. Now he's just a regular firefighter with the county fire department.

But he told me about firefighters who get to travel all around the world helping with flood and hurricane response. And other firefighters who work for the coast guard, sailing the seas (okay, mostly the coasts) in fireboats. There are firefighters working in all areas of emergency response: motor-vehicle accidents, train derailments, even hazardous-material incidents and security threats, like suspicious packages that might contain explosives.

The more E. O. talked, the more firefighting sounded like the career for me. And E. O. did talk — a lot.

When he was finally done his spiel, which included a tour of the fire station and a short ride in one of the fire trucks, E. O. led us into an office with a plaque on the door that read, *E. O. Bouchier, Fire Captain.*

"So, you're actually the *captain*?" I asked as E. O. opened the door and waved Uncle Vic in.

"Yeah. I still assist at the scene of a fire, but more of my time is spent in the station taking statements, doing investigations, writing reports, overseeing staff ..."

"Is it boring?" I asked.

"It can be, especially the political stuff." E. O. still stood at the door, blocking me from joining Uncle Vic. "But my family likes it that way."

"The investigation part must be kind of cool."

"Sometimes. Listen, Hudson, I think you should probably sit this one out. I really need to speak with your uncle. Do you mind having a seat over there?" E. O. pointed to a table littered with magazines, but totally absent of people. Where were all the firefighters? We'd seen a couple under the hood of a truck, one folding hoses and another polishing equipment, but mostly, the place was quiet.

I was about to ask about this, but Uncle Vic piped up from behind E. O. "The kid stays."

"Are you sure? I'm afraid I have to ask you some difficult questions —"

"I don't have anything to say that the kid can't hear."

I felt a prickle of irritation at being referred to first as a "tagalong" and now as "the kid," but the feeling was quickly extinguished by the fact that Uncle Vic was speaking up for me. That he wanted me to stay. It was the opposite of Mom, who always asked me to leave the room or wait outside while she talked to my principal, guidance counselor, Dr. M. ... anyone in a position of authority.

"Okay." E. O. backed away from the door.

I quickly sat down next to Uncle Vic before they changed their minds.

E. O. closed the door behind us and took a seat in front of his computer. "First of all, I have an update on your home."

"Let's hear it," said Uncle Vic. "When can I go back?"

"Well ..." E. O. swiveled his chair away from the computer so he was facing us directly. "It's going to be a long time before you can move back into your apartment — if ever."

"What?" Uncle Vic straightened up in the chair. "Why?"

"The house needs so much work, the owners are considering tearing it down." E. O. paused, letting this information sink in. "But you can go in and get some of your things."

"Good," I said. "Then maybe he'll stop borrowing my stuff." As soon as I finished, I realized I'd made a tactical error. If I was going to learn anything from this conversation, I needed them to forget I was there. Why did thoughts fly out of my mouth like that, without a filter? I should have a two-second delay, like the kind they use on live TV so they can bleep out "inappropriate language."

Uncle Vic laughed. "Well, maybe we can stop there on the way home ... I really need to get my hands on my guitar."

E. O. glanced back and forth between us. "Actually, we'll have to make an appointment, so I can go with you."

"An appointment? That seems like a colossal waste of time." With his fingertips, Uncle Vic tapped the edge of E. O.'s desk to a rhythm only he could hear. "It's not like I'm unfamiliar with the place. And I'm anxious to pick up my instruments. My equipment."

I could almost hear Mom groaning as he said this. Uncle Vic was already taking up more space than we had, and that was without all his music paraphernalia.

"Well, actually, the place is considered a potential crime scene," E. O. said. "No one's allowed in there without supervision."

"Crime scene?"

"That's why I need to ask you some questions." E. O. shuffled through the stacks of paper on his desk and pulled out a pencil.

Uncle Vic exhaled loudly. "Okay, shoot."

"First, I need you to tell me your version of events from the night of the fire."

"You mean *the only* version of events?" Uncle Vic chuckled nervously and then repeated what he'd told Mom. Basically that he'd come home, put on the kettle and then fallen asleep.

"And what kind of kettle was it?" E. O. asked.

Uncle Vic yawned. "The kind that you put on a burner."

"A stovetop kettle?" E. O. checked something off on his piece of paper.

"Yes." Uncle Vic snapped and pointed his finger. "I got it at the thrift shop."

That sounded right — I knew Uncle Vic liked to buy secondhand. Reusing is better than recycling, and all that jazz.

"Okay." E. O. took out a diagram of Uncle Vic's apartment. He put it in front of Uncle Vic and pointed to a box with the word *kitchen* inside, like he was a coach with a play sheet. "So, the fire started here, and you fell asleep on the sofa, here?" He moved his pencil to the box right next to the kitchen, marked *living room*.

"Yeah, that's right. Just like I told you guys before. The fire department and the police. I haven't changed my story, and I'm not going to." Uncle Vic leaned forward. "There's no reason to."

"Well, it's just that some things don't add up." E. O. reached behind his computer and held up a thermos. "Coffee. Want some?"

"Please," Uncle Vic replied, to my surprise. I'd heard him complain just this morning that it soured his stomach. I watched him closely as he stifled another yawn. "Got anything strong to go with it?"

"No." E. O. filled the mug next to his computer and then pulled another mug off the shelf above him for Uncle Vic.

"Didn't think so." Uncle Vic sniffed. "But you can't blame a guy for trying."

"Hudson? You want something?"

As the steam rose from E. O.'s mug, I wished I

could evaporate, too. So much for getting them to forget I was there. "No, thanks."

"You sure you don't want to wait outside?" E. O. tried again.

"With all due respect," Uncle Vic said sharply, "let's just get this over with."

E. O. placed his mug next to the keyboard on a scrap of paper covered in dark brown rings. Squinting, I could just make out the words *musician, drugs* and *record* scribbled there.

Drugs. Could that explain it? The bags under Uncle Vic's eyes? The exhaustion? The erratic behavior? He *was* like the stereotypical user in one of those antidrug videos they showed at school. Would E. O. question him on it? Did I want him to?

"Where were you before you came home that night?" asked E. O.

"I was at a restaurant downtown," Uncle Vic replied, gripping both hands around the mug of coffee like his life depended on it. "I had a gig with my band. A jazzy set for the dinner crowd. There were lots of people. It should be easy enough to get verification — if you need it."

"We have. The owner places you at the restaurant until approximately 7:00 p.m. The band members have corroborated her statement. We have ..." E. O.

glanced at the paper lying in front of him on the desk. "Sage Aaltomaa stating that you left immediately after the band wrapped up."

"Aalto-who? I've never heard her use that name before. She's just Sage."

"Yes, well, Ms. Aal — Sage — is on record as saying that this was unusual. That you usually hang around for a few drinks with the band after a gig. Even the late ones."

"I was tired."

"It was only seven o'clock."

"So?"

E. O. wiped his hands on his shirt, where the words *First In, Last Out* surrounded the fire department's logo. "The restaurant is only five minutes from your house, and the 9-1-1 call was placed at 7:58 p.m. We need to account for your whereabouts between those times."

"There's no accounting," said Uncle Vic. "I came home. I —"

"Did anyone see you come home?"

"I live alone."

"The homeowners don't recall seeing you come home. I understand they live upstairs and rent out the basement?"

"Yes, but it's not like they're in the habit of waiting at the window, watching my comings and goings."

"Okay." E. O. tapped the pencil against his lips. "You came home and then?"

"Took a shower. Put on the kettle. Fell asleep."

"According to our drawing here" — E. O. paused, turning the diagram of Uncle Vic's place so he could see it — "the kitchen is less than five feet from the sofa where you reportedly fell asleep."

"Not reportedly. I did fall asleep."

"There was a lot of smoke. The detector was beeping. How come you didn't wake up?"

"I was really tired. I've been feeling that way a lot lately."

"It's true," I interjected. "I've tried to wake him up — it's tough." I said this because it was the one thing, of all the things that Uncle Vic had said, that I could verify. Not sure why I felt a need to defend him. But I did.

Uncle Vic smiled at me, faintly. "Sorry, kid."

E. O. kept his eyes fixed on Uncle Vic. "Were drugs involved?"

And there it was, like a bomb drop in the middle of an open field. I took a sharp breath.

"Drugs? No." Uncle Vic coughed. "I've never been into drugs. And that's the god-honest truth." With his index finger, he crossed an imaginary X over his chest.

"We have a report that you insisted on collecting

something from your room before exiting the building. A small package." E. O. consulted his notes. "Maybe a pill bottle?"

"Well, yeah, but it wasn't drugs. Nothing illegal." Uncle Vic shifted in his chair. "I just needed some personal items. And my clothes."

But Uncle Vic had left the house wearing only underwear. If he'd had time to go into his room, why hadn't he grabbed a pair of jeans or something? I clamped my mouth shut to stop my surprise from leaking out.

"I'm not here to lay drug charges — that's not my jurisdiction," E. O. replied. "I'm just reporting on the fire, and to be honest, drug use and possession would explain a lot of things."

"Doesn't explain anything because I don't use 'em, and I don't store 'em." Uncle Vic coughed again, louder this time. "Are we done?"

"Almost." E. O. took a sip of his coffee and waited for Uncle Vic's coughing to subside. "The other thing I'm hoping you can help us out with is the lack of ignition material."

"Meaning?" Uncle Vic wiped his nose with the back of his hand — a gesture I'd seen cocaine users make in movies. But I couldn't imagine him doing cocaine. He was always a little out there, but he never seemed high.

"Meaning that if the kettle was behind the fire, then it would have had to ignite something nearby. Without it, the kettle would have just boiled dry. We couldn't find anything."

"Sorry, can't help you out." Uncle Vic rose from his chair. "Maybe there are some things that can't be explained. All I can tell you is that I didn't start the fire on purpose — why would I? It's left me homeless. Without all my stuff."

"Okay." E. O. rifled through the rest of the papers in the file. Was there something else he wanted to ask?

"Speaking of stuff," said Uncle Vic, "when did you say I could pick it up?"

E. O. scrolled through the calendar on his old-fashioned desktop. "How about Friday?"

"Another week?"

"That's the earliest I can get away from the station." E. O. squinted at the computer screen. "One o'clock?"

"Could you meet after school?" I asked. "So I can come?"

E. O. fiddled with the mouse. "I'm not sure that's a good idea ..."

"I was hoping to see what it looks like," I insisted. "Maybe you could explain to me what you look for when investigating a fire? You know, for my report."

E. O. looked up at me with one eyebrow raised. "Well —"

Uncle Vic interrupted. "Friday at one doesn't work for me. How about four thirty?"

"Perfect," I said before realizing that Uncle Vic had addressed his question to E. O. But it was perfect because we had an early practice after school on Friday, which would be over by then.

"Uh ... okay," E. O. said hesitantly. He typed a couple words into the computer and then got up from his desk to escort us out. "Thanks for your cooperation, Victor."

"And thanks for the information, E. O." I shook his callused hand. "I can't wait until Friday."

From the grim look on his face and Uncle Vic's, I knew I was the only one.

CHAPTER EIGHT

After basketball on Friday, I came out of the school buzzing with adrenaline. Adrenaline mixed with a little bit of meds, unfortunately, since I'd had to use my stupid inhaler once (or twice) during the tryout. Still, it had been a great practice. And not just for me. Trev, too.

I hustled toward the spot where Uncle Vic and I had agreed to meet. When I turned the corner and didn't see the car, I slowed down. Planting one foot on the sidewalk, I jumped up and twisted midair, replaying a shot I'd taken over the head of my defender during the full-court scrimmage. I'd been matched against one of the better ninth-grade players — a guy I had pegged as a starter for the senior team. Had Coach Koniuk noticed how I'd beaten him at the line?

Crouching low to the ground, I pretended to dribble. I closed my eyes and tried to imagine the feel of the leather ball on my hand. I faked a pass to the left and then pivoted right. With a pretend pass to my pretend teammate, I executed the perfect give-and-go. When the pretend ball came back to me, I did a spin turn and took one step toward the net for the perfect layup. I opened my eyes, planted my other foot, drove my knee up and was about to release the shot —

I stopped midmotion.

"Still pumped from practice, I see." Willow stood in front of me, blocking the path.

I straightened up and crossed my arms over my chest, sticking my hands under my pits. I wondered how bad I smelled. I'd changed my shirt and added another layer of antiperspirant, but still ... It's not like our junior high had showers. Not the kind that anyone felt comfortable using, anyway. That would have to wait for the big league: high school.

"Yeah, you could say that, I guess." I kicked at a rock with the new high-tops Mom had picked up for me. "It was an okay practice."

"Okay? You look pretty happy."

I smiled, just a little. Truthfully? I loved basketball more and more with every practice. A lot more than I thought I would, anyway. And a lot more than I wanted to with the risk of being cut hanging over me like a scoreboard over an NHL hockey arena. "What are you up to?"

Willow tilted her head in the direction of the gym entrance. "Late practice."

"Oh, yeah, 'course," I said, feeling like a total idiot. I'd seen the other girls warming up on the sidelines as we were cooling down. "Aren't you late?"

Willow shrugged. "I still have a few minutes. Where's Trev?" She took a step toward me and looked around as if Trev might be hiding behind my back or something.

"Walking home," I mumbled as I lowered my head and sniffed, a pathetic effort at discreet underarm-odor detection. "I'm waiting for my uncle."

"How'd Trev do in practice?"

"We spent most of our time on opposite sides of the gym, but I heard someone say that he won a foul shooting —"

HONK, HONK!

The blare of a car horn interrupted me. Willow covered her ears.

"That'd be my uncle."

Willow looked sharply in the direction of Mom's car. "Uh-huh?"

"Yeah ..." I said, although for a moment, I thought about denying it. I didn't want Willow to think he was a dork — sitting in the driver's seat of our old beater, laying on the horn and grinning like Sammy the Banana Slug. On the other hand, I didn't want her to think he was handsome either. What if she started wondering why I hadn't inherited his blond hair and blue eyes?

"Okay, well, see ya," she said.

"Later," I said as she walked away.

"Oh, and you'd better be ready," she called over her shoulder.

"Ready?"

She turned so she was facing me, but she kept walking backward toward the gym entrance. "Firefighting? Our interviews?"

"Oh, I'll be ready ..."

Willow pointed to herself, then to me and then back to herself. "I'm going to put you through the wringer."

I waved her off. Thanks to E. O., I figured I was already well on my way to becoming an expert on firefighting.

Unfortunately, I still had a lot to learn.

❥❥❥

I got in the car, slamming the door extra hard behind me. "You're late," I said.

"I didn't see you rushing to the car." Uncle Vic turned the radio down and started the engine. He never let it idle. I'd heard him lecture Mom about it hundreds of times because she always let the car warm up for ages. She even had one of those remote starters — or environment destroyers, as Uncle Vic called them.

"You didn't have to honk."

"Oh, yes, I did," Uncle Vic said as we cruised onto the main road in front of the school. "You were in pretty deep with that girl."

"Her name is Willow." As I said this, I could see her standing up to Aidan and hear her saying, *His name is Hudson* ...

"She's cute."

"Whatever." I shook my head, erasing the image of Willow's confident smile. "And we weren't in deep. We were talking about basketball practice."

"Oh, yeah?"

"Yeah."

I threw my gym bag onto the backseat, wondering what Uncle Vic would say about Willow's questions about Trev. Why did she care where he was or how he'd done in practice? She hadn't asked me how I did or where I was going.

This was something that an uncle — especially a single one with lots of dates — should be able to help out with. I might've asked him, too, if he'd expressed more interest. But he didn't.

I glanced at him as he sped through the school zone. Even though it was a cool fall day, he wore a faded T-shirt — displaying the logo of some obscure band — and mirrored aviator shades. This style, which had always seemed so cool (especially compared to Mom), suddenly struck me as a disguise. What happened to my hip, rock-star uncle? The one I used to look up to?

When I was younger, we'd hung out a fair bit. But I hadn't seen him much lately. He'd been too busy with his new band — and maybe other stuff as well.

He used to take me on these awesome road trips. Once, we'd made the four-hour drive to Philly to watch the Flyers play the Sabres. Uncle Vic's not much of a hockey fan, but he'd jumped on the Flyers bandwagon that season, and we'd had a great rivalry — until his Flyers beat out my Sabres in the first round of the playoffs.

Uncle Vic had been flush with cash then, and he'd done a few gigs in Wilkes-Barre and Elmira on our way back home. The best part had been camping out at the side of the road, next to a lake. We'd attempted some fishing and then stayed up late telling ghost stories by a crackling fire. Mom would have freaked (and still would) if she'd found out we'd slept under the stars, surrounded by the bears and cougars that lived in the woods. Not to mention the sketchy guys who'd decided to camp there, too, and joined Uncle Vic for a beer. But we'd survived (obviously), and it had been one of the best trips ever.

I reached forward, about to turn the radio up — Uncle Vic had found a classic rock station that was better than Mom's country, but not much — when his phone beeped.

"Is that a text?" he asked.

"Dunno." I glanced at the phone lying on the console between us. "You need to change the settings so it makes different tones for different functions. Sounds like you still have it on start-up mode. You can program it to make different tunes, you know, for each caller. You can even record your own riffs —"

"Just check it for me, okay?"

"Okay," I said, picking it up. "I can program it for you. You don't even have this password protected. Dude, that's just asking for trouble."

"Is it a text or not?" snapped Uncle Vic. "I'm expecting a text."

Without answering, I held up the phone so Uncle Vic could see the text.

CALL ME NOW

Uncle Vic squinted at the phone.

"It's from Sage," I said, remembering the name from Uncle Vic's interview with E. O. "Either it's urgent, or she doesn't know how to take it off caps lock." I laughed a little at my own joke, but Uncle Vic was not amused.

"Sh —" He hit the steering wheel with both hands and then swiveled his head to the left side — the quickest shoulder check in the history of driving. "*Shoot*. I need to find a place to pull over."

The last of my post-practice buzz drained from my body as I twisted the phone in my hand. "Just call her on the speakerphone."

"I can't afford a ticket," growled Uncle Vic.

"You won't get a ticket using hands-free —"

"What?"

"Just call her when we get there," I said, deciding it was easier to simplify things. How did Uncle Vic, who promoted all his gigs on social media, know so little about technology?

Uncle Vic put his foot on the gas. "Doesn't it say call *now*?" His voice dripped with sarcasm — Mom's specialty, not Uncle Vic's. "Not call *later*?"

"If you pull over to call, we'll be late," I insisted.

The phone beeped. Another text from Sage.

NOW! PKG ARRIVED ... GOOD STUFF

"What is it?" Uncle Vic swerved into the bike lane to pass a truck in front of us.

"Nothing," I lied. "Just a reminder about the first text. No big deal." I crossed my fingers and hoped we'd make it there in one piece. And on time, so E. O. wouldn't give up on us. Uncle Vic was worried about getting caught for using his phone while driving, but not for speeding? What about reckless driving? Or arson?

"Do you want me to text back?" I asked. "Tell her you'll call in five?"

"No." Uncle Vic turned onto a side street, tires squealing.

I put my finger over the speaker, hoping to muffle the next beep, and turned the radio up high. A second later, there was another text. I looked anxiously at Uncle Vic, who either didn't hear it or chose to ignore it. Driving along a residential road at high speed — narrowed to one lane because of all the pickups parked along the sides — obviously required a lot of attention. What kind of ticket would you get for hitting a cat or dog? What about a kid?

I took my eyes off the road, even though it made my stomach flip with motion sickness, and read the message.

BUT NO DEX FOR ROX

Package? Stuff? Dex? Rocks? Sage was either really bad at typing or she was using code. Or both.

I gripped the door handle as Uncle Vic peeled around another corner, almost fast enough to make the car go up on two wheels, like a stunt driver.

Sage's texts were suspicious. Was the "stuff" drugs? I once again considered the possibility that Uncle Vic was messed up with something. Addiction could explain a lot. And if he were a user, could he also be a dealer?

We were getting close to his house. I could see blue tarps covering the roof, the edges blowing in the wind ahead of us. "Slow down!" I hissed. "You don't want E. O. to see you driving like this!"

"Chill, kid," Uncle Vic said as he eased off the gas pedal and signaled right, even though there was no one behind us. "It's not like he's a cop. Remember what he said?"

My stomach burned with a toxic mixture of motion sickness and suspicion as Uncle Vic pulled up to the house and then slammed on the brakes to parallel park. "But he knows!"

"Knows what?" Uncle Vic demanded as he threw the car into reverse. "I don't have anything to hide. Not from him!"

The words sliced through me, and I fought to stay

calm. Uncle Vic — a druggie? The more defensive he got, the more possible it seemed. The minute he cut the engine, I jumped out of the car, dropping his phone on the seat behind me.

I could hear him muttering into it through the open car window as I rushed up the sidewalk, but I couldn't make out the words. Not many, anyway.

Okay, I did hear a few: *hook-up, Dex* and *money.*

With each one, a sharp pain dug deeper and deeper into my side.

If it wasn't drugs, what the heck could it be?

CHAPTER NINE

E. O. was waiting near the front of the house, which was damaged beyond belief. Clear plastic covered the front entrance. The door and its frame were gone. All of the windows were smashed, and some of their frames had been cut.

"Hey," I said to E. O. as I approached, still fighting back motion sickness.

"Hi, Hudson." E. O. glanced at the big silver watch that stood out like a beacon on his black wrist. "I'm glad you're here. I was starting to worry."

"Uncle Vic's coming," I said, shoving my hands in my pockets. "Thanks again for including me."

"Don't mention it. Teaching is part of my mandate."

"I know, but with Uncle Vic being under investigation and all ..." I said this to buy time. And also to get the inside scoop.

"Your uncle's not being investigated. The fire is." E. O. kept his eyes fixed on the sidewalk behind me, obviously watching for Uncle Vic. "We have to look at it from all angles."

"Does it usually take this long to figure things out?"

"Not always. Sometimes." E. O. scratched his ear. "It can be a slow process. The answers aren't coming easy in this case, partly because we're extremely low on personnel right now."

"And Uncle Vic isn't exactly being helpful ..." I let my voice trail off, hoping E. O. would fill in the blanks.

"Your uncle's been cooperative. But his story's not adding up. And the insurance investigator is after me for a report. They want evidence of negligence, so they can pursue compensation for the landowner's claim."

The words floated in the air like a ball shot from the three-point line. Time seemed to slow down as I waited for them to sink in. "You mean they want to sue Uncle Vic for the cost of the house?"

"I've said too much. Listen, Hudson, I don't want you to worry about your uncle." E. O. took a step forward so he could see around me, toward the car. "He is coming, right?"

I nodded. "He had to make a phone call."

E. O. rifled through a file folder he had tucked under one arm. "I brought you an information package."

I tried to focus on what he was holding up, but my mind was still processing the stuff about negligence and compensation.

"You know, for your project." He handed me a thick envelope. "My business card is inside. Call me at the station if you have any questions."

"Thanks. I will." As I slipped the package into the front pocket of my hoodie, a million questions ran through my mind. But I knew I wasn't going to get any more information from E. O. Not about Uncle Vic and negligence, anyway. "Can you tell me about fire investigation? Signs of arson? You know, just general stuff for Career and Tech. That class is a killer."

While we waited for Uncle Vic, E. O. gave me a rundown on fire lingo: V-burn patterns (left on the wall when an object catches fire, with the bottom of the V pointing to the source of the fire), irregular-shaped patterns (often caused by puddles of flammable liquid that form on the floor) and flashover (a buildup of heat that causes an entire room to go up in flames).

When Uncle Vic finally showed up, E. O. stopped midsentence.

"Sorry," said Uncle Vic as he stuffed the phone into the back pocket of his jeans.

E. O. checked his watch again. "Okay," he said to me, "I can show you more inside."

"Great!" I followed him around to the side entrance, which was covered with another piece of clear plastic. E. O. pulled it aside, making an opening just wide enough for us to enter.

"You must've made quite an entrance." Uncle Vic laughed nervously as he stopped at the door. Or what used to be a door, before it was smashed to smithereens.

"Try not to touch anything." Broken glass crackled under E. O.'s feet as he stepped further to one side so we could pass.

Before going in, I looked around for the source of the glass and saw the remnants of an upstairs window. "Does the fire break the windows?" I asked. "Or the firefighters?"

"Both." E. O. pointed to a window behind him. "See that?"

I nodded. Hundreds of cracks covered the glass, and there was a single hole in the middle of them, as if someone had knocked a spider out of its web. "Looks like a spiderweb."

"Exactly. Some people actually call it that — spiderweb glass. The technical term is window crazing."

"What causes it?" I asked, resisting the urge to reach out and touch.

"Rapid heating or cooling of the glass." E. O. watched Uncle Vic step into the house and motioned for me to follow without missing a word. "So either the heat from a fast-burning fire, like the kind started with accelerant, hitting a cold window or —"

"Cold water from a fire hose hitting a hot window," I finished.

E. O. nodded his approval.

"And the hole in the center?"

"That was us. We break holes in all the doors and windows so smoke and fumes can escape."

"What about their frames?" I asked as I stepped into the apartment.

"They're cut open to make sure no fire is smoldering behind the woodwork."

"Cool," I said, imagining myself climbing a ladder and jumping through a window into a room full of flames, just like the scene from that old movie *Backdraft*.

"Watch your step."

I stopped inside the door, letting my eyes adjust to the lack of light. "P.U.," I said, holding my nose. Uncle Vic's apartment reeked as bad as the lost-and-found box at the hockey rink.

"Water damage. Often worse than smoke damage," E. O. said. "The neighbors just moved back a couple days ago after the contractor finished cleaning up their place. We had to spray the houses on either side to ensure the fire wouldn't spread."

"Cool," I said again, even though I immediately regretted it when we reached the kitchen and Uncle Vic's contorted face came into focus.

His kitchen, which had never been particularly nice, was a complete and total disaster. The cabinets above the stove were torched. The fire must have spread up the walls from there.

Uncle Vic opened a cupboard on the other side of the room. His head blocked my view of the inside.

"Some things may have been moved," E. O. said, "for the investigation."

Uncle Vic closed the cupboard, coughed and opened a drawer. After rummaging through its contents for a second, he slammed it shut and opened the next one. What was he looking for? It wasn't like his guitar was in there, and I seriously doubted there was anything in this kitchen that could ever be used again.

E. O. moved to the blackened oven. "According to your statement, Victor, the kettle was on this burner here?"

I took a step closer to E. O. so I could hear him over Uncle Vic's cough.

Uncle Vic nodded without looking up. He was digging through a drawer like a dog in search of a bone.

"Was there anything else on the stove?"

"I don't think so. Is it okay if I start gathering my stuff?" Without waiting for an answer, Uncle Vic stuck his head into the broom closet.

"Could the fire have been electrical?" I hoped this was a smart question. It sounded like something you might hear in a TV show like *Chicago Fire*, which was really more of a soap opera than a show about firefighting (the only reason I could ever get Mom to watch it).

"Could be, but electrical fires burn slowly, and this fire was quite advanced." E. O. flashed me a smile that made me feel like his star pupil. A reaction I used to get from my hockey coach — but only when I scored the winning goal.

"So, it was more likely wood?" I asked as I watched Uncle Vic pull stuff out of the closet, seemingly at random: jackets, shoes, a stack of papers, a suitcase. The way he patted down the pockets of his coat and searched the smallest corner of every drawer, I couldn't help but think he was looking for something specific — like a pill bottle.

"It was definitely fueled by the wood catching fire. Yes." E. O. nodded in approval. "But that wasn't the cause. Something had to ignite the wood. The kettle couldn't have done it on its own. We just can't figure out what it was."

"Maybe there was some olive oil nearby?" I ran my hand over the scorched countertop. It felt rippled and rough, like a patch of ice that's melted and frozen over and over again. "He does like to cook."

"But not necessarily tidy up," said E. O.

I surveyed the small room, trying to see it through E. O.'s eyes. I was used to the clutter and the chaos of Uncle Vic's apartment. But even I was surprised by the mess that appeared behind every closed door.

Uncle Vic had finished his search through the closet. He pointed toward the bedroom. "I need to look for my guitar." The rest of the apartment was more like a recording studio than a place to live — he was going to be totally crushed if his equipment looked anything like his kitchen.

"Hudson, you stay here." E. O. led Uncle Vic through the living room. "We'll be quick."

I slumped into the chair next to Uncle Vic's tiny kitchen table, even though it was covered with soot. A stench — like some weird combination of body odor and wet dog — covered everything, but I could smell something else as well. Something acidic, like the chemicals we used in science lab.

I looked around the kitchen again. The stove didn't look like it would ever cook another meal. The oven drawer hung crookedly from its tracks. Chunks of ash covered the floor.

My chest tightened, and I knew I needed to get out of the apartment. The last thing I wanted was another asthmatic reaction.

I stood up and checked my pockets for an inhaler. As I tugged at the information package E. O. had given me, my inhaler fell out and dropped to the floor. I bent over to pick it up, accidently kicking it with my clown-sized sneaker. It skidded across the floor and under the oven.

I dropped to my hands and knees, relieved to find the air close to the floor easier to breathe. The stars floating in front of my eyes disappeared. I pulled open the oven drawer, jerking it up and out until it rolled clear of its tracks. Under the oven, the mouthpiece of my inhaler smiled back at me. I grabbed for it like it was a ball about to roll out of bounds. Even though I was feeling better, I took a puff, staying low, where the air seemed clearer.

Staring at the diamond-printed linoleum, I became mesmerized by the repeating pattern. My eyes followed the black lines that crisscrossed under the oven. That's when I noticed something tucked under the far corner. A piece of fabric. I recognized it; it was from one of Mom's old tea towels. There was nothing left of the cloth besides a small strip of brown and yellow.

"Just a couple more questions to help finish up the report."

At the sound of E. O.'s voice, I got to my feet. He was talking to Uncle Vic.

"Have you received any threats lately?"

Stars reappeared in my peripheral vision as I stood listening. I took a couple of deep breaths, counting each one slowly, the way I did when I was setting up for a foul shot.

"I don't think there's anyone out there who wants to hurt me." Uncle Vic walked into the kitchen carrying a small amp. A huge duffel bag hung across his chest and over his shoulder. But no guitar. "Not since the days of my old band, Scream Soda."

"You were threatened then?"

Uncle Vic shrugged. "It was nothing serious. I never felt we were in any real danger. And we appreciated the publicity."

"Was anyone apprehended?"

"No."

"How long ago?"

"I dunno. I was in college — maybe ten years ago?"

"Probably not relevant, then." E. O. held open the plastic flap and motioned me outside.

I pushed through the plastic and took a deep breath of cold, crisp air. Bile rose in my throat. I started to cough. I couldn't stop.

Stumbling into the bushes, I put my head between my knees. I counted breaths in my head, thinking I had things under control. And then I retched.

"You okay?" E. O. had his hand on my back.

I wanted to push him away, but before I could do anything, I barfed again.

E. O. kept his hand on my back.

When I was sure there was nothing left to come up, I wiped my mouth with the side of my hand and tried to slow my breathing. "Sorry."

"No. I'm the one who should be apologizing." E. O. led me away from the pile of puke and back to the walkway where Uncle Vic waited, casually checking his phone like he was waiting for a bus or something. "I shouldn't have let you inside. There could still be heavy-metal toxins in the air."

"The kid has asthma." Uncle Vic said this like he was ratting on me.

The words *kid* and *asthma* twisted together in my

cloudy brain. I clenched my fists in frustration. I was embarrassed because I'd puked in front of E. O. I was angry that he was the one helping me instead of Uncle Vic.

I dug my fingers into my palm and, without thinking, let out a quiet growl — the same noise I used to make when facing a tough opponent on the ice. In a busy arena, no one ever heard it. But here ...

"Hudson?"

Uncle Vic and E. O. were looking at me like I'd just sprouted horns. And in a way, I felt like I had. I was ashamed, mad and totally fed up with everything: my asthma, my classmates, my family ... Mom keeping secrets was hard enough — but Uncle Vic? I locked my jaw and glared at him, fighting the urge to lash out.

"Hudson?" E. O. said again.

I swallowed. The sour taste of vomit burned in my throat. With a grimace, I turned to E. O. Next thing I knew, I was telling him what I'd found in the kitchen. Never once did I look at Uncle Vic.

"Wow, you've really been paying attention!" E. O. said when I was done. He scribbled something in his notebook and then put it away. "Good detective work, Hudson. I'll get this information to the guys so they can investigate further. I think it could be the clue we've been looking for — I can't believe they missed it."

"I didn't think it was that big a deal." With a shrug, I tried to blow off the praise, even as it melted through the edges of my anger.

"Do you remember what I said about ignition material?" E. O. pointed his index finger toward his temple, signaling me to think. Or maybe he was suggesting that I was smart. Hard to tell. "That could be it."

Uncle Vic raised his hand for a high five. "Well done, kid!"

I punched his hand, hard, releasing some of the tension inside me.

"The kid has strength," Uncle Vic said to E. O. as he shook out his long, bony fingers.

I quickly lowered my fist. I wanted to believe that the kitchen towel explained everything, but I couldn't erase all my doubts about Uncle Vic with one punch.

E. O. checked the time. "Sorry to rush off, but I have to pick up my son. His hockey game is over in fifteen minutes, and I'd really like to catch the end of the third period."

"You're a hockey fan?" I asked E. O. as I followed him around the side of the house.

"Huge," he answered. "I used to play, but now I just watch."

"Who's your team?"

"Blackhawks. All the way."

I felt a stab of disappointment as we continued our single-file trek to the car. Most people who lived in Bluster rooted for the Sabres, but there were a lot of old folks who cheered for the New York Rangers because they were part of the Original Six. There were also hardcore Flyers, Islanders and Penguins fans, because of geography, and some Red Wings and Blackhawks fans, because those were the teams that actually won Stanley Cups. Was E.O. one of those guys who only backed a winner?

"What about you, Hudson?" E.O. asked when we'd reached his truck. "You a Sabres fan?"

"Uh — I don't really follow hockey." My voice cracked.

Uncle Vic shot me a funny look but didn't say anything. Instead he turned to E.O. "Thanks for your help," he said as they shook hands.

"No problem, Victor." E.O. got into his truck. "Good luck with your report, Hudson. If you need more information, or if you have any more clues for us ..." E.O. raised his eyebrows in the direction of Uncle Vic. "Please call."

I gave him a meek thumbs-up before burying my hands in my overstuffed front pocket.

"Oh, and hey —" E.O. slammed the door and started the ignition in one smooth motion. "I might see you at career day."

"What?" I said. My surprise was followed by an unexpected rush of excitement as I pictured the display I was going to put together, outlining all the cool things he'd told me.

"I told my daughter about your project, and it turns out, you both go to the same school," he said. Or, at least, I thought that's what he said. It was hard to make out the words because Uncle Vic was already yelling into his phone, trying to be heard over the roar of E. O.'s F-150 engine.

Before I could ask any more questions, E. O. drove off, leaving us standing on the sidewalk covered in his dust.

Uncle Vic lowered his voice to a mumble. I watched E. O.'s brake lights as they bounced up and down over the speed bumps our car had flown over about an hour ago. My excitement disappeared faster than it had arrived as another set of images flashed through my mind. E. O. practicing with his son on the outdoor rink they made together in the backyard. Going over plays with him before the big game. Cheering for him in the stands. Sharing a plate of nachos with him while they watched the Blackhawks beat the Red Wings on SportsNet.

Uncle Vic turned suddenly in the direction of Mom's parked car. "Guess we'd better get going."

I dragged my feet through the dead leaves piled next to the curb, thoughts of my own dad invading my space. Again. What would it be like to have a dad like E. O.? A dad who came to my hockey games. Or my basketball games. Or my birthday parties. Or anything.

I didn't even know my dad's name.

CHAPTER TEN

"I need to make a stop," Uncle Vic said as we hit the road again.

I visualized the errands Mom used to drag me on after my Saturday hockey games: grocery store, dry cleaner, post office, bank ... It always started at the food court in the mall. We'd replay every goal while I gobbled down something greasy and Mom sipped her second or third coffee of the day. That part was good. But the other stops always took way too long. By the time we reached home, I was bored to death and in desperate need of a shower.

My stomach growled with hunger. Mom would be furious if we weren't home in time for dinner. "How long?"

"Quick. I have to find my guitar and ... I was sure it was at the house." Uncle Vic talked more to himself than me. "Plus, I have to talk to Sage."

"Where are we going?"

"This building up here." Uncle Vic turned a corner,

using his knee and one finger to steer. "A couple of the band members share a studio in there."

"Okay."

Uncle Vic pulled up to a shabby-looking low-rise. He shut off the engine but left the keys in the ignition. "You wait here."

"No way," I said, glancing around at the seedy neighborhood.

Uncle Vic looked irritated as he grabbed the keys. "It'd be faster without you."

I scrambled out of the car. "I'm not exactly slow."

With a sigh, Uncle Vic locked the doors.

"And besides, you have 'nothing to say that the kid can't hear,'" I added, imitating Uncle Vic's raspy voice.

Uncle Vic rolled his eyes but didn't protest as he led the way into the building.

The studio turned out to be an open room with a small, dirty window looking out onto the parking lot. There was a large desk, covered with papers and a couple of ancient-looking desktops, shoved into one corner. An old sofa sat in the middle of the room, with big, ratty cushions scattered around it. The place smelled like the back of the Zamboni shed at the arena — where people (not me) smoked cigarettes and grass (not the lawn variety).

"The rent is cheap," Uncle Vic said as we stepped into the room.

"Uh-huh," I said, trying not to stare at a couple of girls — women, I guess, although they looked younger than Uncle Vic — who were trying to hang a poster. A strange guy, with an unlit cigarette hanging out of his mouth, stood off to one side, supervising.

"Hey, everyone, meet my nephew, Hudson." Uncle Vic twisted his sunglasses around so they were on the back of his head. "Hudson, this is everyone." People around the room nodded and waved.

A woman appeared from behind a curtain of beads hanging in a doorway at the far end of the room. "Hi, Hudson," she said in a soft voice. She was pretty, with long, straight hair and a flowing beaded skirt that swished around her as she moved toward us. "What do you think of the poster? It cost a fortune, but I think it'll get us lots of publicity."

Uncle Vic whistled. "I like."

The poster was blue with white trees in the foreground, and SONIC ENERGY: *Change the Way You Think* was written across the top in huge, bold letters. The details of an upcoming concert were listed in smaller print below. "What's the concert for?" I asked.

"We're raising awareness," said the strange guy,

his cigarette bobbing up and down between his lips. As he turned toward me, I noticed his T-shirt — a marijuana leaf with the words *Free Mary Jane* below. If Uncle Vic's friends were into dope, could they also be into something heavier?

"Awareness of what?" I asked Uncle Vic.

"Isn't it obvious?" he replied.

The possibilities flashed through my mind like advertisements on a Jumbotron. All bad. All illegal.

"Our band believes in sustainability," said Uncle Vic. "That's why we've gone carbon neutral — hey, that should've gone on the poster," he said to the pretty woman with the beaded skirt who stood next to him.

"Keep the poster simple. That's what we all agreed. We can talk about the carbon-neutral stuff during the concert," she replied.

"Right." Uncle Vic winked. "Sage is always right," he said before disappearing into a corner of the room, which was stacked with instruments.

"You're Sage?" I asked awkwardly.

With a smile, she nodded. Her dimple reminded me of Willow's. "You play any instruments?" she asked.

I shook my head.

"You should jam with us sometime. Try a bongo drum or something."

"What do you play?"

"Percussion, mainly. A bit of guitar." Sage ran her fingers through the ends of her hair, making the bangles on her arm jingle against each other. "Mostly I'm the singer."

I wanted to hear her sing.

I looked around the room as Sage and I stood there, waiting for Uncle Vic. I'd insisted on coming up to the studio so I could snoop — but I wasn't really sure what I was looking for. The place certainly didn't seem like one of those drug dens you see on TV. Instead, it was relaxed and friendly, like the dressing room after a win. There was a potluck sign-up sheet posted on the bulletin board and incense on the windowsill. Maybe the weird smoky smell was actually incense — patchouli, the kind Mom hated.

"Found it!" Uncle Vic's voice echoed off the low ceiling as he emerged from the corner.

"Your guitar?" Sage's voice was light and airy in comparison — a bit like Willow's. "Groovy."

"I can't believe it was here the whole time." Uncle Vic brushed some white powder off the side of the case. "Right next to Jasper's sax."

"Groovy," repeated Sage. For some reason, the word sounded cool coming off her tongue — not dorky like it would if anyone else said it.

Uncle Vic swung the case over his shoulder. "Hey, did any of my suggestions pan out?" he asked Sage. "We definitely need a Dex replacement. We're in deep."

Sage shook her head and the beads on her skirt danced. "What about Hudson?"

I suddenly felt light-headed, like I'd just finished two back-to-back shifts on a penalty kill. A side effect of the incense — or something more? Was Uncle Vic using code now, too? Were they looking for a new drug runner or something?

"Hudson?" Uncle Vic frowned. "He's a jock. It's not his thing."

"People don't fit into those kinds of packages," said Sage. "You know that, Vic."

Packages?

"Well —"

Sage raised her hand, cutting him off. "He's cute, and it could help us attract a younger demographic."

Cute? Me? I pretty much stopped breathing.

Uncle Vic set his guitar down next to the door. "The kid's way too tall to sell the cute and innocent routine ..."

Whoa, wait a second. Did they want me to sell drugs at school? We'd been warned about that — pushers hiring kids to sell to their friends. But Uncle Vic wasn't like that. Was he?

"But," Sage insisted, "we need an extra ..."

As Sage and Uncle Vic bantered back and forth, talking about me like I wasn't even there, I tuned them out. Thoughts crammed into my numb, nonworking brain like cars in a parking lot after a game — all moving slowly in random directions with nowhere to go.

My eyes focused on the white powder on Uncle Vic's guitar case. Was that cocaine? Was there so much of it in this "studio" that it hung in the air, clogging up my brain? Or was the woozy feeling just a combination of the incense and my empty stomach? I needed some fresh air.

"I'm outta here," I said through gritted teeth. "I'll see you in the car."

Sage looked at me — concerned. Her eyes were brown and deep. The rushing sound of blood thumped through my ears. I looked down at the floor and then happened to glance at Uncle Vic's guitar case with the white powder on it ...

I charged toward the door, and *somehow* my foot connected with the guitar's black hard-shell case on my way by. Pain shot through the toe pushing at the end of my high-top.

Everything in the room — the movement, the chatter, the music — ground to a halt.

Sage stood there, scratching her head. "Are you okay?"

I rolled my ankle to make sure it wasn't sprained. "I think so," I said, even though I knew I was anything but okay. Only the injury wasn't physical, it was emotional. It seemed like Uncle Vic and his friends were up to something. And I didn't like it.

"Good," said Sage.

Everyone else went back to what they were doing.

Uncle Vic picked up his guitar case and cleared his throat. "Guess we'd better hit the road, eh, kid?"

As Sage kissed Uncle Vic on the cheek, I shuffled out the door as quietly as I could.

A few people called out "Bye, Hudson" behind me. I wondered if one of them was Sage. But having made such a fool of myself, I knew she'd probably never speak to me again. No doubt she was second-guessing the idea of including me in ... whatever.

I dragged my fist along the cracked walls and chipped paint that lined the hallway. Pulling on the rickety handrail a lot harder than necessary, I took the stairs two at a time to gain distance from Uncle Vic. But when I got to the car, I had no choice but to wait for him. Standing there in the middle of the parking lot, I tried to sort out whether I was onto something or actually *on* something.

"You want to talk about what just happened in there?" asked Uncle Vic as he unlocked the car. "You were acting pretty strange."

"No." I slumped into my seat, trying to figure out how to deal with my suspicions. Even though the clues were there, did they really add up? It was still hard to believe that Uncle Vic was into drugs. But what else could explain his weird behavior?

As we pulled away, I looked up at the low-rise and thought I saw Sage's profile in the studio window. "Is she your girlfriend?"

"Sage? No." Uncle Vic smiled. "No. It's not like that. The band? We're like family."

Jealousy jabbed me like the edge of a stick blade. No wonder he no longer paid much attention to me. "Then why don't you just go and live with *them*?" The shot was out of my mouth before I could stop it.

"Look, I know I've crowded you out since I moved in. But I've enjoyed hanging with you, kid ..." Uncle Vic rubbed his chin thoughtfully and took his time choosing his words. "I know I haven't always been the best uncle. Or brother. But I've always loved you guys more than anything. Family really is the most important thing ..."

"Then how come you're never around unless you need us?" *And how come you're hiding things from me?*

I wanted to ask the second question — the more important question — out loud. But I didn't.

"Well, I guess that's because I also love to play guitar. Which means I'm on the road a lot. And lately I've been really into this sustainability thing. I'm sorry. I didn't know it affected you so much, Hudson."

Uncle Vic waited for me to respond. I didn't. After a few minutes, he turned up the radio. "You have to check out the solo on this track. Pure genius."

Music filled the car as Uncle Vic hummed and drummed along. I reviewed what had gone down in the studio. What was the deal with all this sustainability stuff? I'd always assumed that his activism was just an angle he used to get publicity. Maybe that was part of the problem — I didn't know him any better than he knew me.

"Have you always done stuff for the environment?" I asked when the song was over and the station had cut to commercial.

Uncle Vic nodded. "Since college. It started with your mom's campus greening campaign."

Another something — and someone — I knew very little about. Suddenly, I saw an opening in the play. Maybe a backdoor pass could get me behind Mom's rock-solid defense. "Mom was part of a campus greening campaign?"

"Not just part of it; she organized the whole thing. Met with the college administration and convinced them to make a lot of changes: banning pesticides, forcing the cafeterias to stop using disposable dishes and cutlery, setting aside land for community gardens —"

"Mom did all that?"

"Yup. Got me into the campaign when she asked the band to play at a fundraising concert."

"Scream Soda?"

"How'd you know?"

"You mentioned it to E. O."

"Oh." Uncle Vic lowered the sun visor.

"What about my dad?" I hadn't planned to ask, but before I knew it, the words were out there, and I couldn't take them back. I knew they'd all met in college.

"Your dad?" Uncle Vic took his eyes off the road to look at me, even though we were driving through the busy section of town, which led to the freeway.

"Was he involved, too?"

Uncle Vic turned his attention back to driving just in time to see the light change ahead of us. He jammed on the brakes. The car came to a skidding stop in front of the red light.

We sat there in silence as a dad pushing a stroller

stepped around our front bumper in the crosswalk, glaring at Uncle Vic through the windshield. The light turned green, but Uncle Vic didn't move. The car behind us honked.

"All right, all right!" Uncle Vic said, shaking his fist in the rearview mirror.

When the car was rolling again, I took a chance and repeated my question. "Was my dad part of the campus greening campaign?"

"Not so much." Uncle Vic pursed his lips together. "Listen, kid, if you want to know about your dad, you'll have to talk to your mom."

"But you know how she is —"

"I know, kid. I'll try to get her to open up, but it's going to take patience. She'll tell you someday. Everything happens in its own time."

I knew by the set of Uncle Vic's jaw that there was no point asking any more questions. I banged my head back against the headrest and kept my eyes on the road.

The secrets were piling up faster than a heap of dirty laundry: activist mom, missing dad, criminal uncle ... I needed to know more.

Why did nothing seem to happen in my time?

CHAPTER ELEVEN

I had a weird dream that night — weird because I remembered it and weird because it wasn't about sports. Uncle Vic was on stage playing drums (also weird because I'd fallen asleep to the soft strum of his guitar). In the dream, his drumsticks were on fire, burning the words *Scream Soda* onto the side of a drum as he played.

As soon as I woke up, I googled *Scream Soda*. Four million hits, mostly about some kind of rum cocktail. I tried *Scream Soda + music band* and filtered by language and location, but I still ended up with a ton of results. I started searching through each page, hoping to find something about Uncle Vic's college band.

There were two reasons. The first, to research Uncle Vic's connection to drugs. The second, because I wanted to know more about my dad.

Here's the sum total of what I already knew: Mom had met my dad after he formed a college band with Uncle Vic. Mom started dating my dad when she was in med school. Mom dropped out of med school when they decided to have a family. (I'm not sure how much planning went into this decision, but whatever.) My dad left Mom after Darwyn died.

That was more than ten years ago, and no one had heard from him since. As far as I knew.

When I was younger, I asked about him all the time. Mom gave me tiny bits of information but never his name. I'd stopped asking questions because Mom got so weird about it. And because it didn't seem to matter much. Until now.

I surfed for over an hour but didn't find anything — just a bunch of garbage about song lyrics, cream soda and Ozzy Osbourne. I was looking at the website of an electro-rock band from England when I heard a knock on my bedroom door.

"Hudson?"

I slammed my laptop shut. "What do you want, Mom?"

"Just wondering if you're coming down for breakfast. Uncle Vic made pancakes."

As soon as I heard Uncle Vic's name, I knew I'd missed the obvious. I needed to add Victor Pickle to my list of search words. But there was no way

I could do it now. Mom would be suspicious if I missed breakfast.

"Hudson?"

"Uh, yeah, sure, I'll be right down."

"Okay, see you in a minute," Mom said through the door.

I pulled on some new sweatpants, which were already too short to wear in public, and stomped down the stairs. Uncle Vic was sitting at the dining table — wearing his own robe for a change — whistling as he glanced through the paper. In front of him sat a steaming stack of pancakes and a bottle of syrup.

Mom came out of the kitchen carrying the coffee pot. "You okay, Hudson? I heard you up pretty early this morning."

"I'm fine." I sat down and filled my plate with food, disappointed (but not surprised) by the lack of bacon.

Mom filled her mug and then Uncle Vic's. "Lots of homework?"

I nodded as I chewed. I was waiting for Uncle Vic to say something about the damage I'd done to his guitar. Its case was hard — my big toe still stung from the impact — but not exactly designed for full-contact protection.

"You got some good info from E. O. yesterday, didn't ya, kid?" he asked instead.

I swallowed. "Yep."

"Sounds like there's lots of damage to the house." Mom sat down and pointed to the newspaper at the far end of the table. It was open to a page with a headline that read, *House Fire Suspicious.*

The actual article was only a few lines long. It quoted E. O. as saying, "Those old places burn hot and fast." He also complained about the fire department's lack of resources to investigate the fire properly. While the homeowners were described as upstanding citizens, the article made Uncle Vic sound like a shady musician with a criminal record.

I glanced at Mom, who was pouring syrup over her pancakes, carefully, in a spiral pattern. She'd obviously read the article already. Had they discussed it? Argued about it?

"Does this piss you off?" I asked Uncle Vic.

"All publicity is good publicity." Uncle Vic picked up his coffee and then put it down again without taking a sip. He was already finished eating. And Mom thought I ate fast. No wonder he was always complaining about stomachaches. "And I'm sure they'll be able to complete the investigation now that you're on the case."

Mom raised her eyebrows. "Hudson?"

Uncle Vic smiled at me. "Kid's really in deep with the whole firefighting thing."

"In what way?"

"I found a burned-up dish towel," I mumbled through a mouthful of sticky syrup. "Underneath the stove."

"Is that some kind of clue?"

"E. O. seemed to think so," said Uncle Vic.

Mom wrapped both hands around her white coffee mug, her fingers covering the red lettering: *You don't scare me, I'm a hockey mom.* "How did they miss it?"

I shrugged. "It was really far under the stove, and it blended into the floor. I only noticed it because it's the same as ours. Remember the big economy pack you bought?"

"Yes, I remember." She took a sip. "I also remember that you never paid me back for your half, Vic."

Uncle Vic ignored the accusation. "The kid would make a good detective," he said, trying to imitate E. O.

I felt a rush of pride, suddenly picturing myself in the uniform E. O. had worn when we first met.

"Great job," Mom said, still clutching at the mug like her life depended on the heat it provided.

"And you got lots of information for your project?"

I nodded. "I'm getting pretty into it. Finding out lots of cool things about firefighting. Enough to make me think that being a firefighter could be in my future. Maybe Career and Tech isn't such a waste of time after all."

The wrinkles on Mom's face tightened. She chewed slowly through her first bite of pancake, as though she had a mouthful of hockey tape instead of syrupy, buttermilky goodness.

Uncle Vic pushed his chair back from the table. "E. O. asked a couple of questions about the old days, when me and the band got those threats. Remember?"

Mom put down her fork. "Of course," she said quietly.

"Got me and Hudson talking about college. The kid has some questions."

"About college?" A look of relief crossed Mom's face. "This career and technology elective sure has you thinking a lot about the future, Hudson."

"Not my future," I said slowly. Uncle Vic had given me an opening. It was up to me to take the shot. "Your past."

"What do you mean?" Mom asked sharply. The side of her mouth was twitching madly.

"The kid wants to know about his dad," said Uncle Vic, ignoring the anger in Mom's voice.

She stared at the pancakes on her plate as if they'd just jumped up and slapped her in the face.

Uncle Vic and I stared at Mom.

No one spoke.

And then Uncle Vic stood abruptly and grabbed his guitar case from the corner of the room. The scuff mark from my high-top was gone. So was the powder. "I have to go. The band's rehearsing. I'll be gone the rest of the day."

I watched him retreat into the hallway, wishing I could escape, too. I didn't necessarily want to go with him, although seeing Sage wouldn't be bad. I just didn't want to be left alone with Mom. I knew he'd tried to help, but all he'd done was put her on the defense. I'd never get anything out of her now.

I scratched my arm — like it was an itch that was irritating me instead of Uncle Vic — and stared at Mom's hockey mug. I remembered the Christmas it had appeared in her stocking: a present from Santa. She'd opened it with fake surprise but hadn't been able to hide her delight. Mom had always been my biggest hockey fan.

"What are you up to today, Hudson?" she asked

when she was done eating. The pattern of syrup was still traceable on the half-nibbled pancakes that littered her plate.

I shrugged.

"Want to come shopping with me? We're going through a lot of food with Uncle Vic here."

"I have a ton of homework," I said, "and I need to practice." I shot an imaginary ball into an imaginary basket above Mom's head.

She sighed.

Heaviness spread through me as I thought about all those early-morning hockey practices. Me with my protein bars. Her with a travel mug of coffee and a muffin. Mom had never missed a practice or a game. And we hadn't spent much time together since I'd hung up the skates.

But I had work to do.

As soon as the dishes were done, I raced back to my room. My new Google search found an article about a blues band that had played at a bar in Rochester. It wasn't a glowing review, but it did have a list of the band members: Victor Pickle, Fritz Baneck, Chris Lyons and Simon Sadowski.

I tried googling some of the names of the other band members, but that got boring really fast. Before I knew it, I was googling Victor Pickle again.

I started looking at articles that might link him to drugs, but soon I got distracted by other things. His Facebook page. His Instagram account. The Sonic Energy website.

I limited my search to Google images and found a picture of Uncle Vic sitting on a tricycle at a Critical Mass ride, wearing a Sonic Energy T-shirt. I looked at the picture closely, trying to see if Sage was somewhere in the background. What kind of bike did she ride?

The more websites I visited, the more I got to know my uncle. And the more mysterious he became.

His passion for music and the environment was obvious. It was plastered all over the internet like car ads at a hockey rink. But arsonist and drug dealer? I couldn't find anything that even hinted at that.

The fire was probably related to the dish towel, but that didn't mean it was accidental. Could Uncle Vic have started the fire for publicity? He'd certainly pulled a lot of stunts in the past, though I couldn't see his angle here.

And if it was accidental, we still didn't have an explanation for how he'd slept through it.

That brought me back to drugs. I really didn't

want to believe that Uncle Vic could be a user or a dealer, but what about the weird texts from Sage? And the stuff he'd tried to remove from his apartment during the fire? All the strange behavior?

I was about to give up, when the eighty-seventh search result caught my eye. It was an archived two-line article about a group of musicians arrested for drug possession: Victor Pickle, Simon Sadowski, Emile Aguillard and Joseph Novak.

Joseph Novak. The name was just slightly more familiar than the rest. Like the answer on a multiple-choice quiz that sounds just a little less wrong than the others, even though you don't understand the question.

Joseph Novak. My dad?

CHAPTER TWELVE

I spent the rest of the weekend wondering how I could dig up more information about my mysterious — and potentially criminal — family. The internet didn't provide much. People's lives weren't displayed on the web back in the old days, at least not like they are now. The more I searched, the more I ran into dead ends. When my eyes started to blur from staring at the computer screen, I shot some hoops and prepared for my interview with Willow.

For some reason, I wanted to impress her — either by acing the assignment or totally blowing it off. Since I was still kind of psyched about the fire details E. O. had given me (and because I didn't want any more notes going home to Mom), I went for the ace. So I was kind of bummed when the interview didn't happen on Monday. Instead we had another guest speaker, who bored us with details of how his mining company extracts salt from rock. Yawn.

I didn't even get a chance to talk to Willow until the end of class.

"How was your weekend, Hudson?"

"Okay," I said.

Willow put her water bottle into the mesh pocket on the outside of her backpack. It was designed for that, but Willow was the only person I knew who actually used it. "What did you do?"

"Not much." I shrugged. "You?"

"I went to my uncle's citizenship ceremony."

"Was it boring?"

"Not really. He was so happy, and I know he worked hard for it: filling out applications, taking exams and getting all his papers together."

"Papers?"

"Oh, you know, his birth certificate. Record of who his parents are ... that sort of thing." Willow stopped at the classroom door.

"Oh," I said.

Willow smiled.

An idea hit me like a hundred-mile-an-hour slap shot.

"I have to run," I said, even though I'd been planning to ask Trev if he wanted to shoot some hoops.

"Okay, well, see you around," Willow said as she turned down the hall.

I went the other way, making a line drive for my locker.

Why hadn't I thought of it before? My birth certificate. I could find my dad's name there!

❦❦❦

I rushed home, for once happy there was no practice after school. I went straight to Mom's office to look around. The room was small — just the desk and a chair made it feel crowded.

The desk had two drawers. The small one was stuffed with pens, paper clips, a stapler, a set of keys, some envelopes ... nothing exciting. The large drawer was full of hanging file folders. Each one had a label: *Tax Receipts, Visa Bills, House Insurance ...*

Given how secretive Mom was about the past, I didn't expect to find a file labeled *Hudson's Father*. Ditto for my birth certificate. So I went through every piece of paper in the drawer.

Nothing.

I turned to the closet. Mom had designated it "off limits" after I found my Christmas presents hidden there when I was nine. Christmas morning had been a bummer that year, so I hadn't snooped around much since. Until today.

Inside the closet hung a bunch of old clothes,

which looked like they'd fall apart if anyone actually put them on. I pushed the hangers aside. A small silver filing cabinet stood against the wall. I pulled the handle on the top drawer. Locked.

I jumped across the room and grabbed the keys I'd seen in the desk drawer. Seven keys jingled around the ring, none labeled and none that I recognized. The closet was dark and small and hard to move around in, so I fumbled to get the first key in the lock. It didn't fit.

The second key fit, but wouldn't turn.

The third key was in the lock when I heard the garage door.

Heart thumping, I stepped out of the closet and jerked the clothes back in place. I yanked the closet door shut with one hand. With the other, I threw the keys into the drawer I'd left open. I slammed it shut as I ran out the door. Diving onto the living room sofa, I tried to catch my breath. I was about to flick on the TV when Mom came in the door, followed by a whistling Uncle Vic. I dropped the remote like a hot potato and kicked it under the sofa.

"What are you doing, Hudson?" asked Mom.

I stared at the TV. "Thinking."

Uncle Vic shrugged off his jacket. "The TV's not on, kid."

"I couldn't find the remote," I lied. "What are you doing home so early, Mom?"

"Uncle Vic had a follow-up appointment at the respiratory and neurodiagnostic clinic." Mom avoided my gaze as she peeled off her scarf. Uncle Vic fiddled with his thin canvas wallet.

"Follow-up?" I narrowed my eyes at them like a pitcher trying to read the catcher's signal from the mound. I wondered who was keeping a bigger secret — me or them. "Already?"

"There was a cancellation last week, so Uncle Vic got in early …"

"Last week? How come no one told me?" I asked, even though I wasn't exactly surprised.

"There wasn't much to say." Mom kept taking off layers of winter clothing and hanging them neatly in the front closet.

"It was boring, kid. I had to sit around and breathe. Then I had to ride a stationary bike and breathe." Uncle Vic threw a file folder on the coffee table. "I had to take big breaths and little breaths, over and over. I started to feel like I was the big bad wolf terrorizing a bunch of pigs with all my huffing and puffing."

"The first appointment didn't tell us much." Mom smoothed her skirt like she was wiping off a stain.

"We still don't have all the answers, but we do have a little bit of information to share with you."

"What about dinner?" I asked, even though I wasn't hungry.

Mom sat down on the sofa next to me. "It won't take long."

"We'll order pizza." Uncle Vic handed her the phone.

She sighed. "By we, you mean me?"

"Vegetarian, no olives, whole-wheat crust," he sang as he disappeared into the bathroom.

"So, what's up?" I asked when Mom had finished placing the order.

"Well ..." She pulled at a loose thread on one of the cushions. "We were called into the clinic to talk about Uncle Vic's diagnosis."

"Oh." I didn't like the word *diagnosis*. Hockey players were diagnosed with brain injury after multiple concussions. Old people (and sometimes not-so-old people) were diagnosed with cancer. I had been diagnosed with asthma.

"I have this tripsy thing," Uncle Vic announced as he walked back into the room, drying his hands on his jeans.

Mom shot Uncle Vic a nasty look and waited for him to sit down. "It's called alpha-1 antitrypsin deficiency," she said. "The support group refers to it as alpha-1."

"Call it whatever you want." Uncle Vic cracked his knuckles. "This tripsy thing explains my breathing problems, my stomachaches and even the exhaustion I've been feeling. Everything."

Mom cleared her throat. "It's doesn't quite explain everything ..."

"Everything," Uncle Vic repeated.

Tripsy? It sounded more like a cutesy name for a penalty than a diagnosis. "Tripping caused all that?"

"Not *tripping*." Mom bit her lip. "A disease called alpha-1 antitrypsin deficiency."

Disease. Another word I didn't like. "What is it?"

"The liver is supposed to make a protein called alpha-1 antitrypsin," Mom explained. "In someone who has alpha-1 antitrypsin deficiency, the protein is missing."

That didn't sound good. "So, what happens?"

"Other proteins in the body get out of balance ... out of control." Mom twisted the cushion like she was wringing out a dishcloth. "They damage healthy lung tissue and, sometimes, the liver."

"Is it bad?" I asked Uncle Vic.

"I'm not dying. Not anytime soon, at least." Uncle Vic forced a smile, the kind you make when someone takes a team picture right after you've lost the finals. "Don't look so serious, kid."

"Is there any way to treat this tripsy thing?"

"There's nothing they can do to cure it, but they have a team of specialists who can stop things from getting worse," he said.

"As long as you make some changes to your lifestyle," added Mom.

"There are some pamphlets in there if you want to know more, kid." Uncle Vic motioned toward the file folder on the table. "But everything we actually need to know will be explained when we meet with the genetic counselor."

Mom's head snapped back like she'd been punched. "Hudson's not going to that appointment."

"Here you go again." The circles under Uncle Vic's eyes darkened as he lowered his chin. "Putting your head in the sand."

There were red blotches covering Mom's throat. Her face looked sad and distant — the same look she used to get when I was admitted to hospital. "I'm not the one who's in denial," she said.

My mouth went dry. "Why do I have to see a counselor?"

"You could have the tripsy thing, too, kid."

"What?" How could I be sick? I felt fine — mostly.

"Vic —"

"He's a smart kid, sis, and he needs to know the truth."

"One thing at a time." The red blotches on Mom's neck had spread to her chest. "For now, it will just be the two of us seeing the genetic counselor."

"Can't you just see those other specialists you were talking about?" I asked. "The ones who can stop it from getting worse? What's the big deal about genetic counseling?"

Uncle Vic blew out his cheeks. "There's more to it, kid."

My gut knotted. "What?"

The red blotches on Mom's neck were gone. Her entire face was now as red as a match head. "That's enough, Vic." Her voice trembled. "We'll discuss this later."

"He needs genetic testing. And to get testing, he needs to see the counselor."

"It's too early to make those decisions." Mom put her hand on my leg. I could tell she was fighting for control. "I want to discuss the options with a genetic counselor, first. Without Hudson there."

"Why?" snarled Uncle Vic. "So you can control his life the way you control everything else?" I'd never seen him so mad.

"We need more information." Mom's nails dug into my thigh. "I'm taking you to see Dr. M."

My respirologist? Why? Fear bubbled up inside me, but no words came out.

"You just don't want to answer any difficult questions in front of your son." Uncle Vic's knees bounced up and down in the armchair across from us. "Who knows what he might find out about this family!"

"My dad?" I rubbed my arm, suddenly covered in goose bumps.

"This has nothing to do with him," Mom said through clenched teeth.

Uncle Vic flung his arms up in the air. "It's genetic!"

As I watched them go at it, pressure built in my chest like a basketball being pumped full of air. As usual, Mom was trying hard — too hard — to keep me in the dark. But I didn't like Uncle Vic trying so hard — too hard — to blow apart the world as I knew it. One more second of this and I would explode. "Are we done?"

They both ignored the question.

Mom's mouth twitched as she took aim at Uncle Vic. "If you think you can just —"

"I'm his —"

"Well, I'm done!" The words burst out of me. I leaped off the sofa and stormed up to my room, taking the stairs three at a time.

Tick, tick, tick, tick ... BOOM!

.•.

I could still hear them arguing until the front door slammed. I assumed Uncle Vic had gone out. When the doorbell rang, I knew the pizza had arrived, but I couldn't go downstairs. Mom was probably in the dining area alphabetizing her cookbooks. As soon as she saw me, she'd want to have one of her heart-to-hearts: full of feel-good clichés but short on facts.

My stomach growled as I closed my web browser in frustration. I'd found a few sites about alpha-1, but I'd quickly moved on to Scream Soda, Victor Pickle and Joseph Novak. My searches were getting me nowhere. I flopped onto my bed with the laptop and watched the live stream of the hockey game. But it was hard to concentrate on the play.

The Sabres were losing, six to two. Could this day get any worse?

CHAPTER THIRTEEN

"Good answer, Mr. Pickle." Willow pushed back her hair and picked up a pen. She was much better at pretending than I was. Her interview made me feel like a real firefighter. "How did you begin your career with the fire department?"

I cleared my throat and suppressed a smile, totally ready to blow her away with all my firefighting knowledge. "Well, I joined the fire cadet program when I was sixteen."

"While you were still in high school?" Willow tapped the pen against her chin. "How did you find the time?" The way she asked the question, I could easily imagine her as a sports reporter.

I looked down at the stuff I'd copied off the county's website. "It only took one night a week, and it was worth it because I learned a lot about the profession. I also did first aid and CPR courses, and that really helped my application to become a probationary firefighter."

Willow raised her eyebrows. "My aunt works for the police department, and she told me that it's tough to get selected. Almost like winning the lottery. Is it like that for firefighters?"

"You bet," I said, sounding a bit too much like E. O. "There's a seven-step selection process, which includes aptitude testing, panel interviews, a lie-detector test and a physical-ability test." I read directly from the notes I'd copied off an online recruiting manual. "Most recruits don't make it to step seven, which is a conditional job offer. Those who do still have to undergo a comprehensive medical assessment and fitness evaluation that includes a treadmill test."

"Wow." Willow looked totally impressed. "So what kind of person can get through that process? I mean, what qualities does it take to be a firefighter?"

"I'm glad you asked that, Ms. Flores." I was getting into the role-playing, and I was happy that I could quote E. O. directly. "Successful applicants must have strong athletic abilities, be good team players and possess excellent problem-solving skills."

"That sounds exactly like you," Willow said, her dark eyes sparkling in a way that confused me.

"Well, uh ..." I stammered.

"It's such a big responsibility. Saving lives like that. I'm sure you'll be great at it."

Willow was still speaking like a reporter. But she'd said something like that before, when she wasn't playing an interviewer. Did she actually think I'd be a good firefighter — for real?

Heat spread across my face. "Yeah, well, do you have any more questions?" I held up my sheet of notes, wishing it were some type of shield. "I still have lots of answers."

"How did you find out so much?" As Willow flicked the paper between us, the tip of her finger brushed across my hand. "Did you print it all off the internet?"

The paper floated out of my hand and onto my desk. "Uh —"

"You okay?" Willow leaned forward and looked me straight in the eyes, like she really wanted to hear what I had to say.

And so I started talking superfast, as though I was trying to keep up with the blood pounding through my veins. Next thing I knew, I was telling her all about the fire at Uncle Vic's house, my trip to the fire station and E. O. I even told her about the towel I'd found under the oven.

When the bell rang, I stopped midsentence and

took a breath that turned into a yawn. I couldn't remember what I'd been saying, so I didn't finish. Silently, I vowed to never speak again. I was bored of myself. Imagine how Willow must have felt.

But she waited for me to continue. When I didn't, she said, "That was awesome! It's great E. O. helped you out so much." She stood up. "Are you going to practice now?"

"Yeah," I mumbled.

"I'll walk with you."

"Cool." I shoved my desk back into place as fast as I could. "Let's go," I said quickly. I didn't want Aidan to catch up with us.

"Where's Trev?" she asked, not moving as fast as I wanted.

"Dentist."

"Is he coming back for practice?"

"Dunno." I'd asked him the same question, but he hadn't really answered. Trev wasn't exactly warming up to basketball the way I'd hoped. But I did notice that Coach Koniuk picked him to demonstrate plays a lot — more than he picked me, anyway. I wasn't sure what that meant. But I was desperate to know who was going to make the team, so I looked for clues in every little thing that happened on the court.

"So, how do you think tryouts are going?" Willow

asked, like she'd been reading my mind as we walked together. She kept pace with me, which few people managed to do.

I shrugged. "I'll be glad when they're over."

"Me, too," Willow said. "I can't wait for the season to start. I'm *soooo* ready to play a real game."

The comment stung. Willow was so confident, so tall, so coordinated, so ... *healthy.* "I don't even know if I'll make the team," I mumbled. I was suddenly jealous of her. And I hated it.

"Of course you will."

I looked at her closely, but I couldn't tell if she was serious. Had she ever been cut from anything?

We reached the gym. "See you in there," Willow said as she pushed open the door to the girls' changeroom.

"Yeah." I watched her disappear behind the swinging door. I lowered my eyes quickly when I realized I was staring into the girls' changeroom. Not that I could see anything — but still.

I turned on my heel and marched directly to the boys' changeroom.

Jerk, jerk, jerk, jerk, jerk — all for me. All to the tune of Aidan's chicken squawk. What kind of guy stares at the door of the girls' changeroom like a lonely puppy dog?

I dressed slowly, hoping Trev would show up so I didn't have to go into the gym alone. He seemed to tolerate my presence now, and I appreciated his company — even if things weren't the way they used to be.

I heard Coach Koniuk's whistle. I had no choice. I pulled myself off the bench and headed into the gym. Alone.

After ten suicide sprints, and two small puffs on my inhaler, Trev still hadn't arrived. I stood off to one side and waited for Coach's instructions. Willow came up to me wearing an old, baggy T-shirt. She looked kind of cute with her thick hair pulled back in a ponytail, a couple of curls escaping on either side of her face. I silently begged her not to ask another question about Trev.

"I was thinking we could practice together," she said as she twirled the ball on her finger. "Sometime after school, when there's no tryouts."

"Uh, yeah, sure," I said, examining the lines on the gym floor as if I'd never seen them before.

"How about Friday?"

"Friday?"

"And maybe a few more times before Coach picks the teams." Willow hugged the ball to her chest. "Sound good?"

"But you're not worried about getting cut."

"I'm not worried, but you are and I want to help."

"Why?"

Willow laughed. "We're partners and —"

Coach blew the whistle. Willow continued talking, but I didn't hear what she said.

"We're going to start with some box-out drills," Coach Koniuk announced. "I want the seventh-grade guys and gals to work with Coach Johansen. Eights and nines, you're with me."

Aidan suddenly appeared next to us. "Sorry, Wheezy. It looks like Snow White's coming with me."

I opened my mouth to respond, but my voice had suddenly gone AWOL.

Aidan hooked his arm around Willow's elbow. "I'll be your new dwarf." He flexed his bicep. "Mighty."

"Dopey's more like it," said Willow.

I wanted to blow a whistle on the play. Call a technical foul. Something. Anything. But instead I turned and followed Coach Johansen to the far end of the gym.

As I waited in line for my turn to enter the play, I watched Aidan and Willow out of the corner of my eye.

He goofed around.

She smiled.

I tried to look away.

She grabbed a rebound.

He raised his arms in victory.

I cursed under my breath and told myself to focus on my side of the gym.

He stole the ball.

She shot it over the head of her defender.

I bobbled a pass.

Someone called her name.

He hooted and hollered.

I missed an easy layup.

She caught me staring. Smiled at me. I smiled back.

He caught me smiling. Raised his fist. I burned with anger.

The entire practice was like that — horrible. The more Aidan flirted, the better Willow played. The angrier I got, the more I screwed up.

Coach Johansen yelled at me to pay attention. I focused — too hard, too determined — and was called for charging.

Finally, Coach Koniuk blew the whistle. "That's it, folks. Ten suicide sprints. Go!"

I didn't join the stampede to the baseline. Instead, I went over to the bench to get my inhaler. There was a sharp pain in my chest that had nothing to do with asthma. But I took a puff anyway — the thing was almost out of gas. Like me.

Aidan was running next to Willow, trying to egg her into some type of race. "Nine!" he yelled.

Her hair swung back and forth as she ran.

I shook the inhaler and took another puff. Nothing.

Coach Koniuk stared at me.

"Ten!" Aidan did a victory dance at baseline. "First place!"

I jogged to the baseline.

"And Wheezy hasn't even started!" Aidan strutted toward the bench. Toward me.

I squatted to touch the line. As Aidan passed behind me, I stuck out my foot like I was anchoring myself for the sprint. Except I wasn't. I was aiming for something else: payback. For the time he'd tripped Trev in the hallway. For all the lousy nicknames. For flirting with Willow ...

It was the best timing I'd had all practice.

With his nose in the air, Aidan didn't see my foot. I'd like to say he went flying over it and landed flat on his face — but he didn't. Instead, it was his shoulder that hit the ground. Hard.

Aidan rolled over onto his back, held up his wrist

and rotated it in the air. "Geez, Wheezy! I think it's broken."

"Here's hoping," I muttered as I pulled myself into a sitting position.

Coach hustled over. "What happened?"

Aidan jumped to his feet, still clasping his wrist as if it were about to fall off. "Hudson tried to trip me," he announced.

Everyone had stopped running.

I rubbed my ankle where it had connected with Aidan's foot. Tried? I hadn't just tried. I had succeeded. And some part of my stupid brain wanted to brag about it. Who cared if it wrecked my chances of making the team? I wasn't going to make it anyway. "I didn't try to —"

Willow's voice emerged from the circle of sweaty players that surrounded us. "It was an accident," she said. "I saw the whole thing."

Coach Koniuk looked up at Aidan and then down at me. "Hudson?"

Willow stood off to one side. I could see her face from the corner of my eye — it flashed with warning, like a billboard ad: *Don't be an idiot.*

I slowly nodded at Coach Koniuk. "Accident," I said, gritting my teeth.

Aidan narrowed his eyes at me.

"You're both okay," Coach said. It was not a question — it was a command.

"Yeah, sure." I stood up and tested my ankle with my weight.

"You know me, Coach." Aidan released his wrist and pounded his chest. "Tough as nails."

Coach Koniuk glanced at the crowd. "Okay, then, what are you all staring at? Finish your sprints and then hit the changeroom!"

"Yes, Coach!" The chorus filled the gym.

"You're going to pay for this, Wheezy," Aidan muttered under his breath.

"Aidan. Hudson. Go get some ice." Coach pointed in the direction of the nurse's office. "Just to be safe."

"Roger, Coach." Aidan saluted him and immediately started marching out of the gym. "Hi-ho! Hi-ho! Off to the nurse we go ..."

Willow grabbed my arm as I turned to follow Aidan. "Ignore him!" she hissed.

I didn't look at her. I couldn't.

"Thanks," I whispered.

CHAPTER FOURTEEN

For two days, I nursed my ankle, avoided Aidan outside the basketball court and tried to banish all thoughts of Willow from my mind. I succeeded — mostly — until Friday.

"I can't practice after school today," I told her as she slid into her seat for Career & Tech. "There's something else that I, uh, have to do."

Willow raised her eyebrows. "Something more important than making the team?"

Once again, I couldn't figure out whether she was joking or serious. I didn't want her to think I wasn't interested (in basketball). And I didn't want to tell her I was going to the doctor after school. So, instead, I blurted out, "How about this weekend?"

Willow smiled. "It's a date," she said, just as Ms. Lavender stood up to introduce yet another guest speaker.

A date?

I didn't hear much of what the dairy farmer had

to say. I was too busy worrying about spending time alone with Willow. How was I going to stop myself from rattling on like an idiot again?

By the time the bell rang, I'd figured my way out of the *date*. I leaned over toward Willow's desk and said, "Tomorrow? Two o'clock? Meet at the Y?"

"Great!"

"I'll bring Trev, too," I said, even though Trev didn't know anything about it. Yet.

"Okay." Willow's voice changed slightly, like she'd agreed to have lettuce and tomato on a burger because it was healthy. Not because she liked it that way.

●●●

Mom was waiting for me in the parking lot behind the gym. The engine was running as I hopped into the front seat and strapped on my belt.

"Let's go," I grumbled, annoyed that she was dragging me in to see the *pediatric* respirologist. At what height did I no longer qualify as a little kid? I just hoped we were seeing Dr. M. because of Uncle Vic's diagnosis and not because Mom had somehow found out how much I'd been using my inhaler. "I want to get this over with."

When she didn't acknowledge me, I realized she was on the phone, which put me on high alert.

Mom on the phone was very unusual — like a point guard doing a slam dunk. She carried her phone everywhere, an ancient thing that you had to flip open, but I hardly ever saw her use it. Ditto for the home phone and computer.

The heater blasted my face as I slouched down in the seat and waited for her to get off the phone. I thought about Uncle Vic's smartphone and wondered whether he had programmed it yet. Was Sage still sending him cryptic texts?

I hadn't seen Uncle Vic since his fight with Mom. Her story was that he was busy with an important tree-hugging event. My bet was she didn't have a clue where he was.

"Ready?" Mom folded the phone and slipped it into her purse.

I yanked my hat forward to cover my face. "Who was that?"

"Grandma."

I lifted my head in surprise. Grandma called us every couple weeks from New Jersey, mostly to complain that we never called her. She always had some new ache or pain to tell us about, and she always called on the landline. "What did she want?"

"Actually, I called her."

"Why?"

"I just needed to ask her some things."

"Things?"

"About our family medical history."

"Straight up, Mom," I said, frustrated by all the secrecy. "Are we going to see Dr. M. because I've had a few small asthma attacks? Or because I might have Uncle Vic's tripsy thing?"

Mom shivered, squared her shoulders and started the car. "Hudson, just be patient."

"Fine."

We drove to the hospital in silence. I didn't even bother to turn on the radio. I knew if I asked, she would say no.

···

"Alpha-1 antitrypsin deficiency is an autosomal recessive disease," said Dr. M. "Do you know what that means, Hudson?"

Mom squirmed in her seat.

"We learned about it in science," I answered, trying to fast-forward to what really mattered — did I have the tripsy or not? "It means you get one gene from your dad and one gene from your mom, right?"

"Something like that. The gene involved in alpha-1 is supposed to produce a protein. Most of us have two working copies of the gene, so we make more than enough protein to protect our lungs and other organs." Dr. M. scribbled on some paper as she talked, putting capital *A*s next to lowercase ones until a pattern emerged. "Some people have only one working copy of the gene, but they're still okay because the liver can make enough protein with just one. But if you get two genes that don't work, your body can't make the alpha-1 antitrypsin protein at all."

"So my uncle got two busted-up copies of the tripsy gene, one from Grandma and one from Grandpa?" Our science lesson about Mendel's peas, the one I'd failed, was fresh in my mind thanks to the alpha-1 website I'd skimmed through.

"Probably, but —"

"Aren't we getting a little ahead of ourselves?" Mom rubbed her forehead. "We don't have the results of Vic's genetic test yet. I just wanted to mention it to you, so you have all the information. Are we all set with the peak flow meter?"

"Yes." Dr. M. smiled her familiar smile, letting it spread across her face to show she had enough patience for both me and Mom. "Any more questions, Hudson?"

"Do I actually have to carry that around with me?" I pointed to the peak flow meter perched on the desk between us, a familiar contraption that looked like a cross between an inhaler and a test tube.

"We need to make sure we are managing the asthmatic symptoms appropriately. Like I said, the increased reactivity could have been triggered by your recent viral infection, the change in temperature, your growth spurt or a combination of those factors. If that's the case, the attacks should start to decrease, as long as you stay healthy. But it's also possible that we'll have to put you back on medication to avoid overuse of quick-relief inhalers."

"But I really don't want to take it to school."

"Please, just be cooperative, Hudson. You heard Dr. M. It's also possible you're reacting to some dust mites in the gym or something." Mom shuddered.

"So, what if I am? It's not like I'm going to quit basketball," I barked back. I was angry at her for ambushing me at my own appointment — making it about my recent attacks and Uncle Vic's tripsy thing. And then, to make matters worse, she'd shut Dr. M. down before I could get any good information.

"Let's wait till we have all the answers, Hudson." Mom turned to Dr. M. "Can I speak to you for a moment in private?"

"But ... I ..." Frustration blocked my words. I couldn't speak fast enough, or loud enough, to keep myself in the game.

"Please," Mom added, talking over my protest.

Anger turned to rage. When was she going to stop shutting me out? When would I be old enough to have a say in my health? And at what age would she start being honest with me about our family?

Dr. M. checked her watch. "I have another appointment in five minutes."

"It'll just take a moment," Mom replied.

Dr. M. closed my file. "Hudson, do you mind stepping into the waiting room?"

"Fine." I slammed my hands against the desk and pushed back my chair. It caught on the carpet and went crashing backward.

"Hudson?"

Without answering, I turned on my heel and stormed through the door, leaving the chair in its place. Abandoned — exactly the way I felt.

♥♥♥

I paced through the waiting room, too geared up to sit down. When I got close to Dr. M.'s closed door, I hesitated, trying to make out the voices from behind the thick wood.

The receptionist watched closely, probably suspicious of all the noise I'd made when the chair fell. She'd asked if I was okay, offered me some water and finally decided to leave me alone after I snapped at her. But she still had an eye on me.

I clenched and unclenched my fists as I walked, not caring if I wore a hole in the carpet with my heavy feet. I heard the words *Darwyn* and *died* and *affected* and *Hudson* — my name and my brother's were the easiest to pick out because they were repeated over and over again.

A mom and her son came into the waiting room, full of smiles and affection as they sat down to read a book together.

My mind raced as I tried to put things together with the pieces I had. It was like trying to complete one of the puzzles Uncle Vic used to pick up at the thrift store.

Darwyn.

Died.

Affected.

Why were they talking about Darwyn? He didn't have asthma. As far as I knew.

Finally, Mom came out and thanked the secretary. We walked down the hall in silence.

When we got into the elevator, I exploded. "Enough secrets!"

I didn't look her in the eye — I couldn't — but her image reflected back at me in the mirrored elevator walls. "What does all this have to do with Darwyn?"

Mom gripped the handle next to the elevator buttons like it was the only thing holding her up. "Hudson —"

"Tell me!"

"Your brother died of liver disease." Her eyes filled with tears. "Which is also associated with alpha-1."

"He had the same thing as Uncle Vic?"

The elevator door opened. Mom grabbed my shoulder. "We don't know yet —"

"If Uncle Vic isn't the only one affected ..." The facts spun through my brain, faster and faster, like a hamster on a wheel. "Then it must run in the family."

"Hudson —"

"I'm right, aren't I?"

The elevator door closed. We were still inside.

"We *cannot* jump to conclusions," Mom said, squeezing my arm. "We have to wait and see what the genetic counselor ..."

I stopped listening as Mom rattled on about genetic tests and lifestyle management.

Alpha-1 affected the liver and lungs. Uncle Vic, Darwyn and now ... me.

The last piece of the puzzle clicked into place.

I had asthma. A lung condition. And it wasn't going to go away.

Because I had alpha-1, too.

CHAPTER FIFTEEN

I stood in Trev's front hallway, waiting for him to get his stuff together.

Gran handed him his skullcap. "Remember. I'm picking you up at three."

"Okay, Gran." Trev grabbed his bag.

"I like seeing you boys." Gran pushed her glasses up the bridge of her nose. "Together."

"See ya, Gran," I said as I opened the door.

"Bye!" Her hand flapped up and down as she waved.

Trev pulled the door shut behind him.

"She's picking you up at three?" I asked as we walked down his driveway. I wasn't surprised that Trev was bowing out early. What surprised me was how easily he'd agreed to come with me. Still, it didn't leave a lot of time for practice.

"There's this thing at the church."

I made a face. "Can't you get out of it?"

"No," Trev snapped.

We walked the rest of the way to the YMCA in silence.

I kind of wanted to tell him about my argument with Mom and the tripsy and all that, but it was mostly too confusing to explain. Besides, Trev didn't worry about stuff the way I did. Or at least he didn't talk about it.

Willow was waiting in the gym when we arrived.

"Sorry we're late," I said.

"No problem. I was a bit early." She took a ball from the rack next to her and shot it from the three-point line.

Trev whistled as the ball swished through the net. "Nice shot," he said, stripping off the warm-up pants he'd worn over his shorts.

"You have a good shot, too." Willow smiled — not at me, but at Trev. "It just takes practice."

And that's what we did — for almost an hour with hardly any breaks. It was good.

Willow came up with a bunch of new drills, and Trev seemed to get into it. Total understatement. Trev got so into practice that he increased his game by at least 300 percent. He never played that well in front of the coaches. Was he trying to impress Willow?

I pushed that question to the back of my brain,

refusing to admit that the answer might be right there in front of me.

There wasn't much time to chat while we played, and that was good, too. Who knows what I might have babbled about, with Willow nodding and smiling at me? At both of us, actually.

We were playing Around the World when Trev's gran came to pick him up. She invited me to come along, but I said no.

"How about you, Willow?" asked Trev.

"No, sorry," said Willow as she pushed back a clump of hair. "I'm going out with my cousin. But thanks for asking."

As Trev and Gran left, I went to the bench for a drink of water. When I was done, I threw the bottle in my backpack and turned toward the changerooms. "So I guess I'll see you Monday," I said to Willow.

"Are you kidding, Hudson?" Willow took another shot that sailed through the net. "You still need to work on your pull-up jump shot."

"But I thought you had to go."

"I have a little more time," she said with a smile.

"O" — a hard pass hit me in the stomach, making my voice crack — "kay."

And that's how I ended up playing one-on-one against Willow.

***

"You don't have to wait with me, you know," Willow said as we sat on the curb waiting for the bus to the mall. Her cousin was meeting her there.

"I know." I picked up a handful of stones and watched as they dropped through my fingers, one by one.

A bus went by. I started to cough. "Sor ... sorry."

"Got your puffer?"

I nodded, even though I wasn't sure. I hadn't needed it during our practice.

I took off my backpack and started feeling around inside it. After a few seconds of no luck, I started pawing through it faster and faster, worry strangling out what little air I had left. I'd used it the night before, and I didn't remember packing it with my gym clothes.

Willow stood up and kicked some leaves.

I stayed where I was, searching through the outer pockets of my backpack.

"So, what did you end up doing yesterday after school?" Willow asked. "You took off so fast, I didn't have a chance to ask."

My fingers closed around the plastic actuator of my inhaler. I was about to pull it out of my bag when I noticed Willow looking at me through eyes that seemed wider and rounder than usual.

She took a step back, reminding me of all the kids who had given me a wide clearance in the hallway after my asthma attack at basketball — as if I might suddenly come crashing down on them like some old, rotten tree.

Discreetly, I palmed the inhaler and stood up. "Yesterday? Nothing ... just dumb ... dumb family stuff."

"Everyone okay?" Willow fiddled with a ring she'd put on when we'd finished playing.

I nodded. "I don't have much family." I wheezed. "Not like you. Is your cousin cool?"

"Yeah, she's cool. Do you have any cousins?"

"Nah. My uncle doesn't have kids. And my dad, well, you know ..."

"Yeah, I know. How come your mom never remarried?"

"*My* mom?" I coughed, mentally gagging on the impossible image of my mom holding hands with a man. Kissing a man. The idea of her letting someone else interfere with her perfectly planned and boring life.

"It's hard to see your parents with someone else." Willow frowned, reading into my reaction. "But you get used to it after a while."

I wanted to tell Willow that she had it wrong. It

wasn't the thought of Mom with another man that was so shocking. It was the thought of her with anyone. My dad had disappeared so long ago that I didn't remember them together. I didn't have any memories of her with *anyone*. Ever. She didn't even have a lot of friends.

But I didn't say any of this to Willow. I didn't want to look or sound stupid in front of her — not again — so I kept quiet and focused on breathing. *One. Two. Three ...*

"The cousin I'm meeting now is actually the daughter of my stepdad's brother." Willow hesitated. "Or, wait, maybe she's my stepdad's cousin's daughter."

"There must be a lot of them if you can't keep track."

Willow laughed. "Yeah, I guess. We're all just one big, happy family. It doesn't really matter who's related to who. Or how."

"Huh." Every time I exhaled, I could hear the faint whistle of air exiting my lungs — or trying to. But I was determined not to use my inhaler in front of Willow.

"Family is what you make it." Willow spoke in a deep voice with a Spanish accent. "Family is everything!"

"Your dad?" I guessed at the origin of the accent,

hoping I wasn't missing something obvious. Did someone on TV speak like that?

Willow nodded.

We fell into silence as a truck drove past the bus stop.

Exhaust filled my nose, and my chest squeezed shut as I stepped away from the road.

"So ..." Willow fiddled with the zipper of her fleece track jacket. "Have you heard about the Halloween dance?"

I shook my head, even though I'd seen the posters. They were kind of hard to miss — werewolves, vampires and zombies, surrounded by black-and-orange block lettering with lots of exclamation marks. Plus, they were plastered all over the school.

"I was wondering —"

Another truck zoomed by and Willow stopped talking.

"Uh-huh?" I managed to mumble, keeping my mouth closed.

Willow moved the zipper up and down, up and down. "You okay to practice again this week?"

I rubbed my hand over my chest and spoke slowly. "Not sure it'll make much difference."

"Of course it will. You just need the right attitude."

"Attitude?" I kept taking small gulps of air, hoping

she wouldn't notice my distress. Would her bus ever get here?

"Confidence and determination."

"I am determined. It's just that ..." I tried to take a deep breath, and then, with stars floating in front of my eyes, I let it spill — the truth, or at least some version of it. "Look at me. I'm a freakin' giant."

"What's wrong with being tall?" Willow's eyebrows shot up like the arm of a referee. I should've taken the misconduct penalty and gone straight to the box. Instead, words kept coming out of my mouth until I ended up with a game suspension.

"Everything," I wheezed, forgetting that Willow knew nothing about my hockey disaster. "What is it good for, except reaching the top shelf? Average is better."

"Thanks a lot." I felt the air frost as Willow spit the words at me.

My mind raced, trying to make sense of what I'd just said. Or what Willow thought I had just said. Why hadn't I just kept my big mouth shut? "I-I didn't mean —" I stuttered.

"Whatever." Willow's bright face was suddenly as dark as Darth Vader's. "No one can control how tall they are, and I'm tired of being teased about it. So I'm not cute and petite? Big deal."

"But —"

Willow cut me off. "This is me," she said as her bus finally pulled up to the stop, showering us with more exhaust.

She jumped on board as soon as the door swung open. She didn't look back.

"See you Monday ..." I watched the bus pull away as Willow walked down the aisle, looking for a seat.

Then I leaned against the shelter and took a long pull from my inhaler.

As my lungs filled with air, the rest of me filled with regret. What had I just done?

CHAPTER SIXTEEN

Early Monday morning, we had our first big dump of snow. Everyone was running around with their magic carpets, snow runners, GT racers and flying saucers. Even the kids at my school abandoned their cool junior-high personas for quick trips down The Hill, the only hill in town steep enough to slide down.

Everyone seemed happy.

Everyone but me.

Both girls' volleyball teams had home games after school, so we didn't have basketball.

Instead, I invited myself over to Trev's place to play video games. He tried to blow me off, but Gran welcomed me in and even served up some hot dogs with my favorite sauerkraut — homemade from her own special recipe that stunk up the basement every summer.

Even though Trev hammered me on every platform — especially the one where avatars gave out truth points (something he gloated over big-time, pointing out my history of dishonesty) — it was fun. Almost like old times, or at least enough to reassure me that our friendship hadn't totally gone up in smoke.

But then he started asking questions about Willow, and I hightailed it out of there.

First her about him, and now him about her? I didn't want to talk about it. Talking had only gotten me into trouble.

When I got home, I went straight to Mom's office, hoping to do some sleuthing before she finished work. I felt guilty about sneaking around, but finding out more about my dad was like a scab I couldn't stop picking at. Especially now that I knew about alpha-1.

Joseph Novak. Was that really him? I thought so, but I wanted to be sure.

So far, the only thing I'd found on him in my online search was connected to Uncle Vic. Was it possible that he'd disappeared off the face of the earth after he ditched us? Or did someone — Uncle Vic? Mom? — still have contact with him? It was a long shot, but maybe some document locked away in Mom's secret filing cabinet held the information that no one seemed willing to share.

I grabbed the keys from the desk drawer and went

straight to the closet. After getting tangled in some coats, I angled the cabinet so it faced the open closet door. But then my body blocked the office light, making it hard to see the lock. I needed a flashlight. I backed up through the closet door ...

And straight into Uncle Vic. "Hey, kid."

I froze. "What are you doing here?"

"I got back from the sustainability tour this afternoon. I was downstairs in my room, unpacking." He nodded toward the closet. "Question is, what are *you* doing in *there*?"

"Just looking for something." I gulped. "Does Mom know you're back?"

Uncle Vic shook his head. "I made a surprise dinner. It's already in the oven."

I put the office back together as best I could and grabbed my backpack from the floor. I joined Uncle Vic in the kitchen. Pots and pans littered the stovetop. The sink was full of bowls and gadgets from Mom's prized food processor. Almost every cupboard door was open.

It had been one week since Uncle Vic had stormed out of the house, and now he was back, making himself at home as if nothing had happened. I didn't know how Mom was going to react, but for some reason, Uncle Vic being home made me feel grateful

— like the first deep breath after a puff from my inhaler.

"How was the tour?" I asked, pulling at a patch of dark hair that had sprouted on my forearm, seemingly overnight. "How's Sage?"

"Good and good," Uncle Vic replied. "Every concert was a sellout. And Sage told me to say hi. To you."

"Oh." I blushed and then tugged hard on one particularly long hair to cover my embarrassment. I decided to try some more sleuthing. "So ... did you ever find a replacement?"

"Replacement? Oh, for Dex?" Uncle Vic squinted at a cookbook lying open on the counter. "Yeah, a young kid. Did great at backup vocals."

My mind worked its way back to the text messages. Dex? A band member? That explained a few things. Was the Rox a club?

Uncle Vic added salt to a pot on the stove. "How've you been?"

"Okay." I sat down on the stool and threw my backpack on the counter between us. "Mom's going to freak when she sees this mess."

"She's going to freak even more if she finds out that you've been snooping around," Uncle Vic replied as he dug through the utensil drawer. "Did you find what you were looking for?"

"I want to know about my dad."

Uncle Vic continued to search through the drawer, humming under his breath. Finally, he pulled out a large slotted spoon and slammed the drawer shut with his hip. "I already told you, kid, that's between you and your mom. I'm staying out of it."

"But we're family, and the tripsy thing is genetic. So it involves all of us. Including my dad."

"I'll talk to you about alpha-1," he said. "But not about your dad. Sorry, kid."

"I already know about alpha-1. Darwyn had it and so do I."

"Your mom said that?"

"She said that I have to make good choices, so I don't get sick like you. Lifestyle management, she called it."

"So, you know there are jobs you can't do?" A dark shadow crossed his face. "Like being a firefighter?"

It hit like a shot between the pads. "What?"

Uncle Vic put down the spoon and rested his hands on the countertop so we were face-to-face. "Lifestyle management? Things you can and can't do if you have alpha-1? You just told me you knew all about it."

I felt numb. "I thought she meant eating more stuff like that." I pointed to the leafy greens sticking out of the colander in the sink. "I had no idea ..."

"Sorry, kid."

The buzzer sounded on the oven, startling me out of my trance. As Uncle Vic pulled out a casserole, I struggled to make sense of everything. It was like I was watching my life unfold from the nosebleed section.

Once he'd judged the dish to be done and set it on the cooling rack, Uncle Vic picked up his guitar from the open case on the floor and sat down next to me. "Did your doctor actually say you had alpha-1?"

"Yes," I lied.

Uncle Vic bit his lip as he plucked at the guitar strings.

I thought about how he'd disappeared for a week without saying goodbye. Could I trust him? Would he cut me off — just like my dad?

"Do you still talk to him? My dad, I mean?"

Uncle Vic's fingers stopped moving. "No. Why? What do you know?"

"I know a lot," I lied again. "About the band. About the drugs."

Uncle Vic inhaled sharply and then coughed.

"Tell me," I insisted.

"But —"

"Please."

"There's a reason your mom doesn't want you to know." Uncle Vic made silent chord changes on the guitar.

"But I need to know." My voice cracked on the last word. A cough rose in my throat. I swallowed it, trying to erase the similarity between me and Uncle Vic. Coughing, coughing ... always coughing.

"Why?"

My chest felt like it was in a choke hold. I grabbed the inhaler out of my backpack and took a puff, breathing in as much as I could. I didn't use the peak flow meter, either before or after, even though I was supposed to. After a minute, I managed to croak, "Because he's part of me."

"You're a Pickle." Uncle Vic put his hand on my arm. "Trust me, kid. And there's nothing wrong with being a Pickle."

"No one wants *PICKLE* on the back of their jersey!" The words tasted bitter as they burst out and were louder than I'd intended. "I'd much rather be *NOVAK!*"

I studied Uncle Vic for a reaction, but he gave nothing away. Just as I was about to dig deeper, the lock on the garage door clicked open.

I froze.

Uncle Vic jumped up, laid his guitar on the stool

and started throwing things into the dishwasher. I hadn't seen him move that fast since he'd moved in. Still, there was no way he was going to return the kitchen to Mom's magazine photo-shoot standards.

I pulled my backpack off the counter and onto my lap, hiding the inhaler underneath.

It was time to face the wrath of Pickle number three.

CHAPTER SEVENTEEN

"You're back," Mom said to Uncle Vic as she came into the kitchen.

"Making dinner." Uncle Vic waved the fumes from the pot toward his nose. The room filled with a delicious, spicy smell. He ground in some pepper.

"Did you save some trees?" I could almost hear the ice cracking off Mom's words as steam rose from the pot.

"Sure," Uncle Vic replied, his back to us.

She glanced down at his guitar and scrunched up her nose like it was the recorder I'd brought home in elementary school. It was the only instrument I'd ever seen her touch — and that was only to disinfect it.

Uncle Vic sampled his concoction as it continued to bubble away on the stove. "Dinner will be ready in ten."

Mom put the guitar on the stand in the corner — the one that had suddenly materialized after she'd yelled at Uncle Vic about leaving his guitar lying around everywhere — and perched on the edge of the stool next to me. "How was your day, Hudson?"

"Okay," I muttered.

Mom shifted in her seat, uncomfortable, like there were ants crawling up her back. "Why do I get the feeling that I've walked in on the middle of something?"

I shrugged.

Uncle Vic kept his eyes fixed on the stove.

She dug in. "Who's been hanging out in my office?"

"What?" It was my turn to squirm. My backpack fell to the floor.

Mom was too focused on her attack to see the inhaler sitting in my lap. "I can tell that stuff's been moved around."

I knew I was defeated. I looked to Uncle Vic for help — nothing. I made a choice. It was time to be honest. "I was looking for my birth certificate."

"Why?" she demanded. Judging by the sour look on her face, she wasn't ready for honest.

"I, uh, I need it for a science project," I said, trying to think as fast as I did on the basketball court. "We're studying genetics ..."

"The truth, Hudson," Mom said flatly.

"Well, uh —" My tongue felt like it had been pinned down by a champion wrestler.

"I know you don't want me to interfere, sis." Uncle Vic spoke slowly, wrapping the cord around the food processor to the rhythm of his words. "But if you don't give Hudson the information he wants, he'll find it some other way. He's a smart kid."

Mom rubbed her temples. "What information?"

"About my dad."

"Not now, Hudson." She looked at me with tired eyes. "Please."

Something about the way Mom said *please*, like she was begging for mercy, made me back off. "Then let's talk about alpha-1."

She sighed. "I'd rather wait till we've seen the genetic counselor."

"I don't need a genetic counselor to tell me what I already know."

Now she looked like she was going to puke. "What?"

"That I can't be a firefighter." The words sounded fake as they flew off my tongue — I hadn't really allowed myself to believe it. "That I'm going to be sick like Uncle Vic. That I might even die —"

"No!" Mom's eyes flew open, wilder than I'd ever seen them. "No, no, no!"

I'd gone so far, and even though I was shaking with fear and frustration, I figured I might as well finish it off. "Like Darwyn."

"That's not true!" Mom's tired body suddenly came to life. Her back straightened into a stiff line. "What did you say to him, Vic?"

"I thought he knew —"

"You!" Her finger jabbed the air as she pointed. "Both of you! All this jumping to conclusions! It has to stop!"

"But I —"

Mom's glare shot the words back down my throat. She took a deep breath. "We are all going to see that genetic counselor together to get this straightened out. Get everything out in the open. There is so much you don't understand ..."

"Whose fault is that?" I snapped. "Don't you think I deserve to know that I'm sick? That I may die —"

She put up her hand like a crossing guard stopping traffic. "Hudson, you are *not* sick. You —"

"But my brother was sick. My uncle is sick. And you won't tell me anything about anything ..." My voice faded as Uncle Vic grabbed for the box of tissues on top of the fridge.

"It's just ... I ..." Mom wrapped her hands around

her neck like her head might fall off if she didn't hold on. "Oh, god, no ..."

"I'm sorry," I mumbled, regret jabbing at me like a boxer in one of Trev's video games.

The tears flowed down her face, collecting in a stream as she let out a sob. "I can't ..."

"I know it's hard for you, sis." Uncle Vic spoke softly as he handed her a tissue. "You've lost a lot —"

"And I will not lose you!" Mom said to him, jumping up from her seat. "Or you!" She pointed at me with one hand, balling the tissue up against her eyes with the other.

Uncle Vic nodded with understanding. "Maybe it would be better to talk about it later ..."

"Yes." Mom sniffed. "Later. I promise. Okay, Hudson?"

"Okay." Anything to make her stop crying. To make my heart stop feeling so — *tight*.

"I have a headache." Mom put her hands on my shoulders, pushing down on them like she was trying to stop me from growing. "I have to ... I'm going to bed."

When she was gone, Uncle Vic looked around the kitchen and let out a soft whistle. "Hope you're hungry, kid."

❥❥❥

We let the music on Uncle Vic's phone distract us from further conversation while we ate the superhealthy (and not totally disgusting) meal he'd prepared. I blocked out all thoughts of firefighting and dying and Joseph Novak by concentrating on Uncle Vic's interpretation of each tune. He described songs like they were sports plays and musicians like they were professional athletes.

"Want to shoot some hoops?" he asked when we were done.

"In the snow?"

"Sure, why not?" He pushed his stool away from the counter. "I'll clear up later."

I glanced out the window. "But it's dark. And cold."

"I thought you wanted to practice."

"But what if I fall and twist an ankle or something?"

"Lighten up, kid." Uncle Vic grabbed his coat. "It'll be fun."

And he was right. It was fun. Fun enough to make me think that basketball on ice, with no penalties for roughing, hooking or tackling, should be an actual sport.

"Next basket wins," gasped Uncle Vic as he slid

away from the net with the ball under his arm. Dribbling was impossible on the snow-covered ice, so we'd been carrying the ball around like a football.

"No fair!" I stood in front of him, guarding the net. "You have possession."

His laugh turned into a cough. "The sick guy needs a handicap."

"Oh, no you don't," I said as I tried to poke the ball away from him. Uncle Vic was a much better player than I thought he'd be. Not that either of us would have wanted a scout watching as we lunged and spiraled around the driveway.

"He fakes left," Uncle Vic said as he faked a pass to some invisible player on the left. "He fakes right."

I shadowed the ball with my hand. "Just shoot!"

Uncle Vic leaped into the air and spun around. When he'd almost done a complete turn, he let go of the ball. As his feet hit the ice, they shot forward in front of him, and he landed hard on his butt. The ball sailed up into the air and over the backboard.

"Air ball!" I yelled when I saw the grin on his face. I ran toward the back of the net and fell to my knees, sliding the rest of the way to the ball, which had landed in a snowbank. In one swift motion, I grabbed the ball and shot from where I was on the ground.

Swish.

"The kid has done it again, folks!" Uncle Vic continued his commentary, still sprawled out on the icy pavement. "He's snatched the game away from the favored opponent in the final seconds of the game."

Laughing, I shook Uncle Vic's hand and then plopped down next to him. "Good game!" But my smile disappeared when I noticed the dark circles under his eyes. "You look a little beaten up."

"I'm tired," Uncle Vic admitted. "Damn genes."

"Alpha-1?"

"Probably."

Guilt crept through me like the cold from the ice we sat on. "Is it going to stop you from doing a lot of stuff?"

"It could control your life. If you let it." Uncle Vic leaned forward and rested his elbows on his knees. "But listen, kid, your mom is right. It's possible that you don't have it."

"Is it?" I didn't want to hear any lies from Uncle Vic. I didn't want him to try and make me feel better. And I definitely didn't want him talking in riddles like some kind of shrink. "What about *you*? Is it going to stop *you* from doing stuff?"

"Not really." Uncle Vic rubbed his hands together. "Smoking is the big thing."

"You don't smoke."

"No, but some of the band members do, and it's still in the clubs after hours."

"What are you going to do?"

"Pay attention to where I'm hanging out. Maybe start an antismoking campaign. You know the saying, when life hands you lemons ..."

"Make lemonade," I said with a shiver. "I hate lemonade."

"Me, too." Uncle Vic stood up and held out his hand. "I think I have frost butt. Let's get some hot chocolate."

"Sounds good."

⁹⁹⁹

As we sat at the counter, Uncle Vic told me about a letter-writing campaign he was working on in conjunction with a benefit concert. "Want to help out?" he asked. "It would be great if you could bring it into the school. Get the students involved."

"Sure," I said, thinking about Willow. And next thing I knew, I was telling him all about her.

"She's kind of like Sage," I said, taking a sip of hot chocolate.

"Pretty then?"

I was about to object — a lie to cover my

embarrassment — when Uncle Vic started to cough.

Still hacking, he stood up and grabbed something from the pocket of his jean jacket, which hung, dripping, off the back of the stool. Not even trying to be discreet, he went over to the sink, opened a bottle and shook something out into his hand. He brought his fist to his mouth and then took water directly from the faucet and swallowed. Repeat. He was popping pills — it was as obvious as the fakes my old teammates used to broadcast from the blue line.

"Are those for your cough?" I asked, doubt hanging from every word.

Uncle Vic tapped the pill bottle against his palm, raised his hand to his mouth and threw back his head to swallow another handful. "No."

"Alpha-1?"

"Not exactly."

"I thought you didn't do drugs," I snapped.

"I don't." He turned off the tap. "Not the illicit kind, anyway."

My temper flared. "What is that supposed to mean?"

"Illicit, you know, as in illegal." Uncle Vic returned to the stool next to me. "Drugs are illegal. I don't do drugs."

"Then what is that?" I demanded, with enough force to let him know I was serious. Very serious. I thought about the truth points the avatars collected in Trev's video game — how many could I collect from Uncle Vic? It was time to put on some real pressure and see.

"Prescription medication." He set the empty bottle on the counter. "For my stomach."

I looked closely at Uncle Vic, trying to determine whether he was being straight. I decided to give him a full truth point — he had a bottle plastered with a pharmacy label, after all. Proof. "Is that what you got out of your room the night of the fire? E. O. said it was a small package."

"Yes."

"It's just medicine?" Were his stomach problems so bad that he'd rather risk his life staying in a burning house than go one night without his pills? Surely, he could've gotten the prescription filled again the next day. Mom had gotten a new inhaler at the pharmacy in New Jersey when I'd forgotten mine on a trip to see Grandma. Mentally, I took away half the truth point. "From the doctor?"

"Kind of," he replied sheepishly.

"The truth, Uncle Vic." I could hear Mom's tone of voice as the words slipped out of my mouth.

"The doctor gives me a prescription." He hesitated, measuring me with his eyes like he was determining whether I was a worthy opponent. "But I exceed the maximum dosage, uh" — he cleared his throat — "regularly. So I have to get, uh, creative."

I peered at him as if my eyes held some kind of lie-detecting power. "You're in that much pain?"

"A lot of the time. Without the painkillers, I can't even sleep." Uncle Vic rubbed one eye with the back of his hand. "They really help."

Truth point. "So, why don't you talk to the doctor?"

"I have. I will. Knowing about the alpha-1 stuff will help us get it sorted."

Another truth point. "You think it's related?"

Uncle Vic nodded.

Reluctantly, I gave him another truth point. But he was being too secretive to make it to the next level. "What do you mean by 'creative'?"

"I have my ways." He held up his hands like he was under arrest. "Probably best if you stay out of it."

"Illegal, then?"

"Maybe. Sort of." Uncle Vic cracked his knuckles. "But I do not do street drugs, kid. I never have and I never will. That's what messed up your dad. I'm not going down that road."

"But I saw an article. Online. You were arrested for possession." My mouth was so dry, I could barely get the words out. But I had to — it was now or never. "You and Joseph Novak."

"Joseph?" Uncle Vic inhaled sharply and then went silent. I waited him out by staring at the countertop, focusing so hard that the dots in the laminate started blending together.

"Okay, here it is," he finally said, laying his hands on the counter like he was showing me a losing hand of cards. "Your dad did a little of this and a little of that when we were in the band together. Got us all into a bit of trouble. When you were born, he went clean. But the thing with Darwyn? Well, it really messed him up. He got into the hard stuff then, and it was all downhill from there. He gave up custody, and your mom changed your name to Pickle. I haven't heard from him since."

My gut knotted as the truth points flew around the room. "Downhill?"

"He became an addict."

My stomach sank down to my gangly knees. "An addict?" To me, an addict was someone with bad teeth and skin who lived only for his next hit, like the lowlifes they show in the movies. That was my dad?

"I'm sorry, Hudson."

I sat back, dumbfounded.

Uncle Vic finished off his hot chocolate in one swig. "But listen, kid, what I just said? It stays between you and me. I've probably gone too far. Your mom would be furious."

My mind was rushing to catch up. "But ..."

"It's not my place." He got up and cleared our empty mugs. "I'm not your parent." He grabbed the top of my head across the counter and shook it gently, messing my hair the way Mom sometimes did, only different.

I didn't duck away.

"Although sometimes I wish I was," he added quietly.

With my hair standing on end, I whispered, "Me, too."

CHAPTER EIGHTEEN

"So you can't be a firefighter." Trev stuffed his mouth with a forkful of noodles. "What's the big deal? It's just a project for Career and Tech. It's not like they'll give you a failing grade a decade from now when they find out you're not doing the job you researched. That you're a janitor instead."

He laughed at his own joke.

I did not.

We were sitting in the hallway eating lunch in front of our lockers — Trev's idea. For some reason, he'd decided to take a break from his gaming buddies. And I was relieved not to be hiding out behind the stacks in the library for a change.

So far, I hadn't even touched my sandwich. I'd been too busy filling him in on what had happened the night before. I hadn't meant to spill it all, but Trev had started asking about Willow — again — and I needed something to change the subject.

Talking about my lung disease and probable death seemed to have done the trick.

"Ha-ha," I grumbled, stifling a yawn. I'd been up late, trawling the net for information on alpha-1 and career restrictions. Trev obviously didn't get how interested I'd become in firefighting. It had started as an accidental choice, but now I couldn't imagine myself doing anything else. But if Trev didn't get that, I wasn't about to explain it to him.

Trev closed his thermos. "What about sports?"

I took a bite of ham and cheese. It didn't taste right. "Huh?"

"Alpha-1 affects the lungs, right?" Trev reached into his lunch bag and pulled out an apple. "And exercise stresses the lungs. So maybe lifestyle management means no sports."

"Sh —" I dropped my sandwich. "Shoot."

"So, what are you going to do?"

"Nothing." I banged the back of my head against the locker. "There's nothing I can do until we see that stupid genetic couns —"

I stopped talking when I saw Aidan's shadow looming over us. "What's this about genetics?" he snarled. "Are they using your DNA to make a clone of Big Foot? Or is that experiment still in the rat phase?"

"There's only one rat around here, Aidan," Trev said as he polished his apple with his shirt.

"That's not a very Zen-like thing to say, Mr. Kung Fu," Aidan sneered.

"What do you want, Aidan?" Trev asked.

The metal edge of the locker dug into my spine as I hunched over. Was Trev actually standing up to Aidan?

Aidan looked surprised as well. "You two coming to practice tonight?"

Trev and I spoke at the same time, only I said yes and Trev said no.

"See you at practice then, Wheezy. I'll look for you hiding out behind your girlfriend. It's really too bad that Willow's too tall for a *real* man to want her."

I was too mad to speak. Did Aidan know what I'd said to Willow?

Trev threw his apple core into the bin on the other side of the hall — a three-point shot. "A real man like you?" he asked with a chuckle.

"Be careful, little boy." Aidan dragged a knuckle along the lockers above our heads as he walked away.

"Whatever."

Why was Trev suddenly acting like a superhero?

"And as for you, Wheezy" — Aidan turned and punched a fist into his open palm — "you better watch your back. I haven't forgotten about that trip."

"Do you boys have somewhere to be?" The lunch monitor had appeared around a corner. She bounced as she walked, moving through the halls quickly.

"I do." Aidan flashed a grin and turned on his heel. "Somewhere far away from this fairy tale." Humming "hi-ho, hi-ho," he walked away, arms swinging.

"Everything okay?" The lunch monitor peered at Trev and me over the top of her glasses.

"Yup," I said.

"Fine," agreed Trev.

"What the?" I said when she and Aidan were both out of sight.

Trev slowly put his thermos into his lunch bag. "What?"

"Why are you so gutsy around Aidan all of a sudden?"

Trev shrugged. "I figured out he's not so tough."

"Since when?"

"Since he joined the Roundhouse." Trev was struggling to keep a straight face.

"He's taking martial arts?"

"Yep. And he's awful." Trev started to laugh. "He tried to break a board and almost broke his hand. He looked like the cartoon character from that ninja iPhone app, hopping around, swearing at the wood for not breaking."

"How come I didn't know about this?"

"Since when do you care about what happens in the dojo?"

I ignored the dig. "Do you get to fight him?"

"No." Trev's freckles seem to glow with pride. "I get to teach him."

"I thought you couldn't teach without getting your second-degree black belt?"

"I need the second *dan* to become like Sensei." Trev looked pleased that I'd remembered, making me glad I'd paid attention. "Right now, I'm an assistant instructor."

"Awesome!" I clapped him on the back. I knew how hard Trev had worked for this — he deserved the recognition. "So you get to boss around all the white belts like Aidan?"

"We're definitely not supposed to think of it as 'bossing around,' but it is pretty fun to watch Aidan learn with the other beginners, who are mostly little kids."

"I wonder why he's taken up karate."

"I overheard his mom say something about self-discipline and knowing her son needed more of it as soon as he started potty training."

We both laughed as we put away our lunch bags. But when I opened my backpack and saw my gym clothes, I stopped. "What's this about not going to practice?"

"Oh, yeah. I meant to tell you. Gran's letting me spend extra hours at the Roundhouse, but I have to take confirmation classes in exchange."

I banged my head against the locker door. "More karate *and* Sunday school?"

"Except confirmation classes aren't just on Sundays," Trev said. "So, no time for basketball."

I ran my hand over my hair, trying to flatten it. It sparked with static electricity from rubbing against the locker. "But —"

"We both know that basketball is not my sport."

"But I thought you were into it — the way you agreed to practice with Willow and me ..."

Trev's eyes narrowed like he was focusing in on a target. "I did that to find out what was going on between you two."

"You like her!" The words came out so loud, they startled me. "I knew it!"

Trev's voice rose to match mine. "Me and Willow? No way, man. She's way too tall for me."

Another crack about her height. Was Willow right? Did everyone give her a hard time about it? Being tall was tough enough. But it seemed like being a tall *girl* was even tougher. "What, then?"

Trev raised his hand, and for a minute, I thought he was going to karate chop my head off. "Listen, I was being a, uh, friend."

"You were?" It was the first time in a long time that he'd referred to me as his friend.

"She'd be good for you. Someone else to talk to. You know, about your disease and stuff."

What he didn't say was someone besides him.

"Girls like that sappy stuff," he added.

"B-but she hates me," I stammered.

"Geez, Hudson. For someone who analyzes stuff so much, you really have trouble seeing the forest for the trees."

"What?"

"Something Gran likes to say," he said. "Probably a religious thing."

"Okay ..." I was confused, again. Time to get back on familiar turf. "But what about basketball?"

"Why do you care about that? It never bothered you that I didn't play hockey." He stood up.

"It's just that —"

Trev and I stopped talking as a group of ninth-grade girls walked past us, shuffling their feet and snapping their gum. I recognized one of them from basketball, but she didn't even glance my way. As they swung open the side door, they let in a blast of arctic air that made my lungs contract.

I coughed.

Trev shifted his weight from one foot to the other. "Hey, I heard the Sabres won in OT last night."

"Really?" I got up slowly, shaking out the cramp in my leg, shocked that I'd missed the game. I couldn't believe I'd been surfing the net instead of cheering on my team.

"You didn't see it?" Trev slammed his locker door. "They're playing the Bruins tomorrow. We should watch it together."

"Cool."

Trev and I bumped knuckles. "I'm going outside," he said. "Coming with?"

"Nah, I'm going to the library," I said.

"Catch you later, then."

And for the first time in a long time, I knew I had a friend. No matter what sport he played.

❧❧❧

I walked toward the library, biting the inside of my cheek every time I passed someone in the hallway. After Aidan's threat of retaliation, I felt like I needed eyes in the back of my head — or helmet, as my old hockey coach used to say.

Here's what I knew: Trev didn't need basketball to stand up to Aidan; he had martial arts. But me? I needed help.

Plus, Trev was wrong about me and Willow. But he was right about one thing: I couldn't see anything straight anymore, forest or trees.

Uncle Vic had given me a lot to think about last night, and I guess I believed him. But after so many years of secrets and half-told stories, I still didn't have the full picture. Where was my dad now? Did he have alpha-1? Did I?

I sat down at a computer and googled *Joseph Novak*. Way too many hits without adding another term, like *Victor Pickle*. I tried *Joseph Novak + drugs*. I skimmed the results — nothing obvious. I thought for a minute and then tried *Joseph Novak + addict*. On the third page, I hit on something gold. Not first-place-medal-at-the-Olympics gold, but secret-buried-treasure gold — as in a huge find so totally unexpected, it made you wonder why you'd started searching in the first place.

There it was, laid out in pixels. A low-resolution photograph of a man who looked Eastern European. He had dark eyes, chiseled cheekbones and a small, flat nose that looked exactly like mine. Holding my breath, I double- and then triple-checked the caption: *Josip Novak, Odyssey Addiction Treatment Center.*

The first name was spelt differently. But Josip could be Croatian for Joseph.

It was definitely him. My dad.

Bile bubbled up my throat.

I clicked on the picture.

An article about new addiction services for homeless people popped up on the screen.

I skimmed the contents, praying to Trev's God that Josip Novak was one of the counselors and not one of the addicts. But, of course, he wasn't.

Glancing nervously around the empty library, I quickly shut down the browser and erased the history. The last thing I needed was Aidan — or anyone — finding out that my dad was an addict. And not just a pot-smoking musician or a successful lawyer who snorted cocaine at parties. The stereotypical homeless, down-and-out addict I'd imagined when Uncle Vic had first said the word.

How was that for getting a full picture?

CHAPTER NINETEEN

By the tenth suicide, it felt like a boa constrictor was giving me a hug. But I kept going. I was determined to finish, and I was determined to finish first. I had to do something to prove myself to the coaches. Friday was decision day, just three days away.

As hard as it was, I had to forget about everything — Josip Novak, Victor Pickle, Willow Flores — and concentrate on basketball. With alpha-1 lurking in my genetic makeup, it might be the last sport I ever played.

I leaned over to touch the free-throw line and pivoted quickly. I crossed the baseline less than a second ahead of my closest competitor.

Without celebration, I sprinted straight to the bench. I stopped and bent over but still couldn't catch my breath. Hands shaking, I searched for my inhaler. Since the last attack, I'd kept my puffer close to my water bottle during every practice. And I knew I'd brought it out of the changeroom, even though Trev hadn't been around to remind me.

I searched underneath the bench. Behind it. Where the heck was my inhaler?

I concentrated on breathing. With slow, shallow breaths, I could get enough oxygen into my lungs — almost. Trying not to panic, I looked around the gym. Where could it be?

Most of the players were still running, but Aidan was not. He was staring at me. "What's wrong, Wheezy?" he asked when he caught my eye. "You need another trip to the nurse's room?"

I searched my brain for a comeback, but there was nothing there except for the urgent plea for air. That's when I noticed Aidan was hiding something behind his back.

"My puffer," I said. The words came out too quiet. I started to cough.

"What's that, Wheezy? Speak up! You're talking like one of the dwarves."

Gasping for air, I thought about Trev and imagined Aidan in karate practice, paired against a two-year-old wearing diapers. With a whoop, the toddler flung Aidan over her shoulder.

I pointed at his chest.

"Oh. Are you looking for this?" Aidan pulled his arm out from behind his back and displayed his prize.

As he squeezed the inhaler into his palm, it felt like his hands were wrapped around my throat, choking me. "I found this on the floor of the changeroom. Is it yours?"

I lunged forward and grabbed for his hand.

Just in time, Aidan pulled it back out of reach. "You don't look so good. Should I call the coach?"

The floor wobbled as I glanced across the gym to where the coaches were busy with their clipboards, waiting for everyone to finish running.

I grabbed for my inhaler again, and this time, Aidan let go.

I took a puff. Then another.

"Looks like I saved you from another trip to the nurse's room, Wheezy."

I've never wanted to hit someone so bad. I wanted to punch him right in the face and send his smirk into oblivion.

I took a deep breath and felt the air fill my lungs. I clenched my fists and narrowed my eyes at the target.

But I didn't strike.

Here's what I knew: Aidan wanted me to hit him. But getting into a fight was not going to help me make the team. And neither was ratting him out to Coach Koniuk.

I turned and walked into the changeroom. I sat down and waited until my breathing stabilized. Then I pulled my backpack out of my locker and put my inhaler into one of its deepest pockets. Aidan would never find it there. But I would. If I needed it.

When I went back into the gym, the guys and girls were in separate huddles, getting feedback on the last drill and instructions on the next. I stood just outside the circle surrounding Coach Koniuk and tried to catch up with the plan. Sounded like some type of layup drill.

"Okay." Coach Koniuk clapped his hands. "Coach Johansen will divide you into teams."

Coach Johansen called out the names. But he didn't call mine.

I stood there, in the middle of the gym, while everyone else went to their assigned baskets.

Coach Koniuk turned to me. "Can I talk to you a minute, Hudson?" he asked.

"Sure thing, Coach." I tried to ignore the fire in my stomach as I followed him to the bench.

"I need to check in with you." Coach Koniuk folded his arms across his chest. "I need to make sure your asthma isn't going to stop you from playing competitive basketball."

The fire flared up into my throat. As I stood there

in front of the coach, speechless, I thought about Trev's comment about alpha-1 and sports. Was it already happening?

"We only have so many spots on the team, and I've noticed you struggling —"

"Until last spring I played AAA hockey." The words tumbled out before I realized I'd cut him off. "Captain of my team. Never missed a shift."

"Why'd you quit?"

Sweat dripped down the back of my neck. "I-I —"

"Fell in love with basketball?"

"Something like that," I said because I wasn't about to tell him that I'd lost my coordination. Or any of the other stuff my hockey coach had said.

"Okay. Well, we'll see how it goes." Coach Koniuk scratched his head. "You better get out there. You need to work on your layup."

"Right. Thanks, Coach."

"You can join that group." Coach Koniuk pointed to one of the baskets.

I felt a wave of relief when I saw that Aidan wasn't there. But then I realized that none of the other guys were there, either. It was a group of girls. Including Willow.

❧❧❧

Willow passed me the ball.

I picked it up and dribbled once. I drove toward the net, planting my inside foot. I took one big step and thrust my knee upward. At the top of my jump, I released the ball over my head with a flick of the wrist, just like I'd been taught at summer camp.

Well, not exactly like I'd been taught. I was too far forward. The ball hit the side of the backboard and fell straight back down without even touching the net.

Willow grabbed the rebound and followed me to the back of the line. I gestured for her to go ahead. She ignored me. Didn't even look me in the eye. We watched as two more players passed into the key, drove for the layup and followed up for the rebound.

Neither of us said anything as we waited for another turn. I thought about apologizing for my "freakin' giant" comment. I *wanted* to apologize. But for some reason, I couldn't.

When the next set of girls were finished the drill, they slotted into line behind us. Willow immediately turned her back to me and started chatting with them.

"Are you going to the Halloween dance?" asked a girl whose name I couldn't remember. Willow was friendly with all the basketball girls, anyone athletic it seemed, but I didn't know who her really good friends were. And hadn't really thought about it. Until now.

"I'm totally going," giggled another girl, Lucy.

"I probably will, too," said Willow. "We'll see."

"I'm dressing as Jane — you know Jane of the Jungle?" Lucy's voice bubbled with excitement. "And I'm hoping Liam will be Tarzan!"

"Cute," Willow said.

Lucy and Liam going to the dance as Tarzan and Jane? It was cute enough to make me gag. There was no way I was going to that stupid dance. Even if someone did invite me, which they never would.

My stomach turned as I stared at the floor. Maybe I was getting the same stomach problems as Uncle Vic. I certainly had the exhaustion.

"What about you, Jas?" Willow asked the other girl.

"Oh, I'm going solo," gushed Jas, "as the bride of Frankenstein."

"Maybe you'll meet your groom at the dance," suggested Willow.

"Maybe!"

"I heard Jake and Felicity are going as Popeye and Olive Oyl," giggled Lucy. "Felicity ordered their costumes online!"

"That's a big commitment." Willow laughed.

"Hope they're still together then."

"If not, she'll just have to find a replacement Popeye," said Jas. "I'm sure Aidan would fill the costume nicely."

"*Jasmine!*" Lucy kept her voice low as a sneaker squeaked across the floor.

Willow chuckled softly.

"I think most people are going to the dance in groups. With friends," said Lucy. "Not as couples."

"What about you, Willow? You looking for a date?" asked Jas.

Angling my head slightly, I strained to hear the answer.

"No," said Willow. "I —"

Coach Johansen clapped his hands. "Willow! Hudson! You're up!"

My body jerked to attention.

"We need less chatting and more concentration!" yelled Coach Johansen.

Heat seared my face. "Go!" I hissed at Willow.

"I'm open!" Willow said over her shoulder as she ran into the key.

When she was almost three steps from the net, I bounce-passed the ball so it was just in front of her. Willow grabbed it off the paint and drove in for a perfect layup.

I collected the ball while she waited for me under the basket. Her anger was obvious from the curl of her lip. This was my chance to apologize: *Sorry for being so stupid.* I rehearsed the lines in my head like I was visualizing my next play on the court. *There's nothing wrong with being tall* and *Tall is awesome, especially for a girl.*

But as I jogged toward her, the words evaporated.

"Don't look at me like that," she snapped.

"Like what?"

"And don't talk to me like that, either!"

"Like what?" I repeated as we joined the line again. "I just wanted to — "

This time Willow pushed herself in front of me. "Save it, Hudson." She squared her shoulders and didn't say another word. Not to me, anyway. She did ask the person in front of her if they could switch places. So she wouldn't have to be partners with me again.

I stood there burning with embarrassment and utterly confused. It seemed like I'd done something else I needed to apologize for. But what?

CHAPTER TWENTY

I don't know how I got through the next few days. But I did. And they were awful.

At home, Mom and Uncle Vic tiptoed around each other. It was like living in a museum. The genetic-counseling appointment was on Monday — Halloween — which really got my imagination going. Did the clinic have a lab that created interspecies hybrids like a human-brained giraffe with bear claws and a shark's jaw? Could they tweak some genes to make me smarter? Better at basketball?

I'd been doing tons of homework and studying to get caught up. To play school sports, you needed to have good marks (and make the team). I tried not to think about that (making the team).

Career day was Saturday, so I'd started working on my display board. Again, I needed a good mark, but I also kept hoping Uncle Vic's version of lifestyle management was wrong. If he could be a musician and hang out with smokers, surely I could be a firefighter and hang out in a fire station, with only the occasional visit to an actual fire, right?

I'd almost convinced myself — until I read the recruitment manual.

I needed some information to beef up the corner of the board labeled *Firefighter Qualifications*. I put down my bold black permanent marker and searched my desk for the envelope of papers E. O. had given me. I found the recruitment manual and started flipping through it.

I'd already read most of it, but at the end, I found a section I hadn't seen before. The list of disqualifying medical conditions caught my attention immediately. I skimmed through it, expecting to see alpha-1, but praying I wouldn't. It was kind of like knowing an opposing team was going to win, but hoping for an upset.

What I didn't expect was this: *Unacceptable medical conditions include reactive-airway disease requiring bronchodilators, corticosteroids or anti-inflammatory therapy.*

Right away, I knew what this was — a fancy way of saying asthma. I could almost hear Dr. M.'s voice in my head saying the words *bronchodilator* and *airway disease*. Heart racing, I read through it again, looking for an exception for childhood asthma. Instead, it said this: *The applicant must be without symptoms or medication for two years.*

Anger flared in me like a newly lit match. I might be able to fool Mom, but there was no way I was going to fool a recruitment officer. My asthma alone was enough to prevent me from becoming a firefighter.

With a burst of adrenaline, I threw the manual toward the window. The *thunk* it made as it hit the frame and rebounded onto the bed did not make me feel any better.

I picked up the tri-fold foam display board Mom had gotten at the office-supply store and jumped to my feet. I raised it above my head and smashed it over the corner of the desk.

It cracked down the middle but didn't break.

I hit it against the desk again, full force, snapping it in half. I slammed the two pieces against each other and threw them to the ground.

Still didn't feel any better.

I grabbed the inhaler hidden behind my bedpost. "Stop telling me what I can and can't do!" I yelled as I threw it across the room, this time hitting my target.

The inhaler exploded as it hit the double-paned window, the metal cartridge separating from the plastic case.

"Is everything okay, Hudson?" The sound of Mom's anxious voice seeped through the door.

A grunt escaped from somewhere in the back of my throat. *"Leave me alone!"*

"Honey? Can I come in?"

Each of her words burned into me like disinfectant on an open wound. "I said, leave me alone!"

"I want to help."

It used to be that when I got mad at Mom, I imagined my dad. In my imagination, he was perfect — and everything Mom was not. But now that I knew he was an addict ...

"No!" I yelled at the door, kicking my bed to emphasize the point.

"But —"

"Just go away!"

I thought about confronting Mom with what I knew about Josip Novak. But the memory of the meltdown she'd had the night she'd skipped Uncle Vic's dinner (and the quiet sobbing I'd heard from her bedroom several times since) kept me quiet. Besides that, I was busy trying not to think about him. I had enough to deal with already.

After a few minutes, I heard her footsteps fade down the hall.

Like someone had just pulled the plug, the energy drained out of me and I slumped into bed. Kicking the manual onto the floor, I slunk under the covers. And that's where I stayed for the rest of the night.

CHAPTER TWENTY-ONE

Our last practice went on forever, and everything about it was weird. There were no girls there, just the guys. We didn't do suicide sprints to warm up, just laps around the gym. And we didn't do any drills, just multiple games of one-on-one. Each coach had a list of who was supposed to play who, and they walked around making notes on their clipboards during every matchup.

The pairings weren't random. The final cuts were still being decided, and everyone knew it. We were all out to play our top game.

With only six baskets in the gym, we couldn't all play at once, so there was time to catch my breath between games.

At first, I tried to guess the meaning behind each matchup — like when they started me out against a ninth grader who I'd pegged for starting center. I decided it was because I was the only guy tall enough to block his jump shot — which I did, but only occasionally, and not nearly enough to win or even keep it close.

After a while, I stopped thinking and just played. It was my last practice, and I wanted to make it a good one. So I found a rhythm and stayed there, no matter who I was paired against. I concentrated on getting my shots, driving to the net and making sure I boxed out my opponent — limiting them to one shot and taking things one rebound at a time.

I won some and lost some, and I didn't use my inhaler once.

At the end of the practice, the coaches let us play full-court five-on-five while they consulted over their clipboards.

Finally, Coach Koniuk blew the whistle. "Okay, guys, bring it in!"

"The moment of truth," Aidan said, passing me on the way to the bench. "It's been fun playing with you, Wheezy!"

"I want to thank you all for your hard work during tryouts." Coach Koniuk rubbed his hands together. "We had a difficult decision to make. I wish we could keep every one of you."

"Quit it with the sappy stuff, Coach!" Aidan yelled. "Just tell us who made the team."

Coach Koniuk shot Aidan a look like the one I'd

seen Gran give Trev when he took too many sausages at dinner.

"Coach Johansen will post the junior team, and I will post the senior team. The list will be up on the wall when you're done getting changed. For those of you who didn't make it, I hope to see you out again next year."

Coach Koniuk didn't look up from his clipboard, but I was certain he was talking to me.

"And for those of you who did make the team," Coach Johansen added, "let's make this a championship year for the Cougars!"

There was a chorus of "Yeahs!" before everyone dashed to the changeroom. I grabbed my backpack off the bench and trailed along behind.

Inside the changeroom, a few of the ninth graders were laughing and talking about their plans for the weekend, clearly certain they'd made the team. The eighth graders concentrated on getting changed as quickly as possible. I assumed they were anxious to know if they'd be on the junior team or the senior team. The seventh graders were mixed. Some looked terrified, some looked relaxed, but all of them were getting changed fast. Except me.

I took my time. I wasn't anxious to relive the experience of being cut.

When I finally exited the changeroom, there was a wall of guys surrounding the list. Over the tops of their heads, I squinted at the list for the junior team. Mentally detaching myself from the yapping around me, I ran down the list of names.

Trevor Bach was there.

But not Hudson Pickle.

I did a one-eighty and forced myself to walk toward the exit, even though I wanted to run. With every step, I ranted in my head: *I will not lose my cool. I will not lose my cool.*

Basketball was a stupid sport.

What was the point of running up and down the court, over and over, trying to get a stupid ball in a stupid net? Ditto for hockey.

Anyway, sick people like me probably shouldn't play sports. And firefighting? Who needed a career when you were destined to die young?

I will not lose my cool. I will not lose my cool.

As I pushed open the gym door, my eyes started to water. I quickly wiped my face and tried to convince myself that I was allergic to the janitor's pine-scented cleaner. I didn't want anyone to think I was crying.

I had prepared myself. I had told myself to expect

this. But I was still shocked. I couldn't really believe it was happening.

I will not lose my cool.

And Trev hadn't even shown up for the last few practices!

How did he make the team, but not me?

I will not lose my cool.

CHAPTER TWENTY-TWO

"So, what are you going to do?" Trev asked as we stood next to our display boards.

Career day was almost half over, but this was the first time we'd talked. The area around his display had been crowded all morning. He'd set up his laptop with an interactive game-creator program. It let you do some very basic programming, which everyone thought was totally cool, even the parents and teachers (although they pretended to be more interested in his flowchart outlining the pathway to becoming a video-game developer).

Only Mom, Uncle Vic and Ms. Lavender had come to see my taped-up poster. It showed the steps to becoming a firefighter but nothing else (no pictures, no charts, no nothing).

I honestly didn't care that Trev's display was more popular. It was like asking people to pick between watching the New York Knicks or a junior boys' basketball game. No contest. Plus, the last thing I wanted to talk about was firefighting.

The second-last thing I wanted to talk about was basketball, but I knew that's what Trev was asking about. I gritted my teeth against the anger still smoldering in my stomach from the day before. "I already told you. I'm starting karate."

I'd spent all night convincing myself that martial arts would be fun. I never wanted to try out for anything ever again, and karate was the obvious answer, especially since Trev was going to be there. But still ... I loved competitive team sports. It was hard to imagine my life without them. "What are you going to do?" I asked him.

Trev shrugged. "Coach must've thought I was sick for those last few practices. I'll talk to him on Monday. Free up a spot for someone else." He looked over at his booth. It was getting busy again. "Maybe it will be you."

"Maybe," I grumbled before intentionally changing the subject. "Are your parents coming today?"

"No," said Trev. "But Gran is."

He didn't sound upset, but I felt bad for him anyway. Trev's parents probably hadn't even set foot inside our new school. Had they ever watched one of his karate bouts? Maybe that's why he had taken it so hard when I'd chosen hockey over the martial arts tournament.

"I'll watch for her," I said as Trev went to help someone with his program.

"Hudson!"

I spun around and ended up face-to-face with E. O. "What are you doing here?"

"My daughter goes to this school, remember?" E. O.'s thumbs were tucked through the belt loops of his jeans — it was startling to see him wearing something that wasn't plastered with the fire department logo. "So I thought I'd come see your display. I didn't realize that there'd be so many businesses and community groups with stands, too. It's open to the public, right? I guess that's why they hold it on a Saturday."

I wanted to add, *And because there's nothing better to do in Bluster on the weekend.* Instead, I just said, "Oh."

"Your presentation's a little ..." E. O. scratched his head. "Uninspiring? I'm surprised — I was expecting big things. You seemed really keen."

"That's because I'm not exactly inspired."

"Maybe I didn't give you enough information. Those manuals are pretty dry." He studied the board. "I've got some stuff in the truck that might help. Be right back."

I paced back and forth in front of my display as

I waited for E. O. I'd spent all morning avoiding people: Trev, Willow, Aidan, Coach Koniuk, all the other students, all the other teachers ... and now I had to deal with E. O. When would this day be over? When would junior high be over?

I heard E. O. return before I saw him. He was kicking a box across the floor ahead of him and lugging some type of uniform behind him. He made a shuffling, scratchy sound, like a hockey player dragging his equipment up a flight of stairs.

I ran to help. "You keep this stuff in your truck?"

"I did a school presentation yesterday," he said, nodding to the box of pamphlets.

I picked up the box and led the way back to my display. E. O. followed, carrying the uniform — all fifty pounds of it. Heads turned from every direction, something E. O. was obviously used to and comfortable with. Unlike me.

For the rest of the afternoon, the area around my poster was the place to be. E. O. stayed and explained to people that a firefighter's uniform was also called personal protective equipment or structural turnouts (because the pants get left tucked into the boots, so firefighters can step right into the uniform). He let people try it on, including a couple grown-ups.

It was amazing how psyched everyone was about it, especially my classmates' younger brothers and sisters.

The only ones who weren't impressed were his daughter (who I didn't recognize) and son (who I did recognize — he played in the high school hockey league). They left early, after E. O. called his wife to pick them up.

When career day was over, I helped E. O. take the stuff back to his truck.

"Need a lift?" he asked as I took his helmet off my head.

"No, thanks," I said. "My friend's gran is coming to get us."

"Okay ..." E. O.'s hand was on the handle of the truck door, but for some reason he wasn't getting in.

"Thanks again," I said.

"No need to thank me. Like I said, education is part of my mandate. Seeing all the local businesses and professional organizations in attendance made me realize that we should've been here anyway. We're just so short-staffed."

"Are you any closer to finishing the investigation on Uncle Vic's place?"

"Yes!" E. O.'s eyes lit up. "And actually, I'm the one who should be thanking you, Hudson. That dish towel you found under the stove was all we needed to close the case."

"It was?"

"Yeah. The kettle must have boiled dry on the stove with that greasy towel right next to the element. It just took a little spark to land on the towel and ... BOOM!" E. O. flung his arms up in the air. "So, the investigation is complete, and the insurance company has its report. They're not going after your uncle."

"How did the cloth end up under the stove?" Suspicion pecked at the corners of my brain like a bad habit. Was it still possible that Uncle Vic had been negligent?

"We don't know for sure, but there are lots of possible explanations — all of them part of a plausible accident scenario."

I wasn't sure exactly what a plausible accident scenario was, but if it was good enough for E. O., it was good enough for me. I was done doubting Uncle Vic.

"You did a great job putting it together, Hudson. You may have what it takes to join our team one day," said E. O.

I swallowed hard. "I can't be a firefighter."

His mouth dropped open. "Why?"

"You can't be a firefighter if you have asthma," I said drily. "It's in the manual."

"But people can grow out of asthma," said E. O. "I did."

"You?"

"Yes."

It took me a minute to take this in. "But my asthma doesn't seem to be going away." I kicked at some ice that was clinging to the mud flaps of E. O.'s pickup. "And I also have this thing called alpha-1."

"Oh?" E. O. scrunched his eyebrows together. "And you're sure this is something that will stop you from firefighting?"

"Yeah. Well, I dunno." I shrugged. "I'm still sorting it out. But it seems like my lungs need to stay away from smoke. Even more than most people's."

"Well, if smoke exposure is the problem, there are other careers in emergency services."

"Like what?"

"Like police officer, paramedic, SWAT team member, coast guard, bomb diffuser ..."

An involuntary smile spread across my face as I listened to E. O. ramble off all the jobs that used the same set of skills and strengths that a firefighter needed.

"Wow," I said when he'd finished. "That's quite a lot."

"Well, I can tell you even more, when the time is right." He held out his hand and I shook it. "You let me know if there is anything I can do to help. Ever," he said.

"Thanks."

"You're a good kid." E. O. nodded. "We need people like you."

❧❧❧

I walked into the gym rubbing my hands to get the feeling back in my frozen fingertips. Everyone was packing up. I headed toward Trev's booth with my head down. As I passed by Willow's display board, I heard her laugh. For some reason, I stopped. I felt like I was in the zone — the way I get when I'm playing a sport by instinct and not letting my brain interfere.

As I waited for her to finish talking, I looked at her display board. It wasn't graphic or interactive like Trev's, but it was much brighter than mine. Kind of like Willow herself — full of information (some of it a little confusing) and pretty and cheerful and fun.

"What do you want, Hudson?" Willow said when the girl she'd been talking to finally walked away.

Ignoring the frostiness in her voice, I said, "Great job. Your display makes mail delivery sound like a good career."

"That's because it is," Willow said sharply. She took down her poster.

"Yeah," I said quickly. "There are lots of cool careers here."

"How would you know? Have you looked around?" Willow's hands were on her hips as she stared down at the box she'd put her poster in. "You seem kinda out of it. You walked by here three times before stopping."

"I'm sorry."

"For what?"

"Being a jerk." I hung my head. "For the comment I made about being tall ... for everything."

Willow dropped her hands and looked at me with an expression I didn't understand. Sympathy? Disgust? Something else?

She wasn't saying anything, so I started to yammer, "I don't think you're too tall — not at all — in fact it's one of the things ... It's just that my height got me cut from hockey, and I'm still kinda mad about it. Plus, I found out some stuff about my dad ... and there's this disease I probably have. Or I guess it's a sickness. Well, more like a kind of condition ..."

Willow put her hand on my arm. "You're sick?"

My skin tingled under her touch. "Sick? No — not really." I wasn't sure why I'd brought that up. As an excuse? Or because I really wanted to talk to Willow about alpha-1?

"What, then?"

"Well, it's complicated. I'll tell you more, later. Right now, I have to go catch a ride with Trev."

"Oh, okay." Willow picked up her display mailbox.

I could still feel a tickly pressure where she'd touched my arm. "Do you need help with that?"

"I think I can handle it," she said, puffing out her chest. "After all, I did make the senior basketball team."

"Oh." The wave of contentment I'd been riding since E. O.'s compliment crested and crashed. "Uh, congratulations."

"Thanks!"

Jealousy flooded through me, followed by shame. I'd been so focused on myself that I hadn't thought about whether Willow had made the team. Still, the thought of basketball and my own failure was so painful that I turned away.

"Hudson?"

"I'll, uh —" I swallowed hard. "See ya later."

And I walked away, forcing myself, once again, not to run.

CHAPTER TWENTY-THREE

"I've reviewed the autopsy." Karen Ferenci, the genetic counselor, handed Mom a thin file folder.

Mom reached across the table and took it. She opened the folder just enough for me to sneak a glance at the name on the medical record. Darwyn Novak. "I don't need to read it," she said, slamming the folder shut again.

"Can you just tell us what it means?" asked Uncle Vic. The three of us were lined up in a row across from the genetic counselor, Mom sandwiched between Uncle Vic and me. The room was about the size of a janitor's broom closet.

Karen cleared her throat. "Darwyn died of obstructive jaundice —"

Uncle Vic interrupted. "In English, please."

"It's the type of liver disease that can affect babies with alpha-1," said Karen. "Obstructive jaundice can be caused by other things, too, but now that we have the results of your genetic test,

Victor, we can conclude that Darwyn had alpha-1, as well."

Uncle Vic cracked his knuckles. "If Darwyn had the same disease as me, why don't I have liver problems?"

"Good question. The answer's a bit complicated," said Karen. "Basically, different changes to the gene lead to different forms of the protein being produced —"

"Or none at all," Mom chimed in, like the smart kid who knows the answer before the teacher asks a question.

"Right." Karen pointed to the family tree she'd drawn with circles for women and squares for men. Uncle Vic's square was filled in because he'd inherited two nonworking copies of the alpha-1 gene. Karen had filled in Darwyn's square just before she'd started talking about the autopsy. "Different changes — gene mutations — lead to different symptoms."

"Plus, other factors," Mom said, determined to be the annoying class genius, "like the environment."

Karen nodded. "Mainly cigarettes. If a smoker has alpha-1, they will typically develop respiratory disease in their forties or fifties. If you don't smoke, symptoms can be delayed until sixty years of age or older. In fact, there are some individuals with alpha-1 who never develop symptoms at all."

"I used to smoke, but I'm not even close to forty, and I have lung damage already," said Uncle Vic.

"There are other genetic and environmental influences, most of which we don't understand." Karen pointed to a graph that meant nothing to me.

"So what do we know?" Uncle Vic's fingers fidgeted over the table as though they were plucking at invisible guitar strings.

Karen smiled, making her eyes disappear into her face. "For a person with alpha-1, the incidence of lung and liver disease increases with age. We can reduce the risk of disease through lifestyle management and, in some cases, more intensive treatment —"

"Like what?" demanded Mom. "Intensive how?"

In a reassuring voice, Karen told Mom about the option of a liver transplant and something called augmentation therapy. But I wasn't listening to any of her *CSI* lingo — I was focused on those words: *lifestyle management*.

"What does lifestyle management mean?" I asked when I thought Karen was done — or at least close. "Can I still play sports?"

"Of course," she answered. "Exercise helps keep

the lungs healthy. We actually recommend physical activity to people with alpha-1."

Score one for the good guy. Not that it mattered — I'd already been cut.

Still, I psyched myself up to ask one more question. The big one: "What about firefighting?"

"What about firefighting?" Karen repeated, looking a little confused.

"Can people with alpha-1 be firefighters?"

"Well, part of lifestyle management is avoiding exposure to smoke and other environmental toxins, like mineral dust and gas. Also, occupational pollutants such as fumes from —"

Cutting her off, I said, "So the answer is no."

"Let Karen finish, Hudson." Mom squeezed my knee underneath the table.

"I probably wouldn't recommend a career in firefighting for someone who was affected," Karen said slowly, "but —"

"Never mind. I knew it." I pushed Mom's hand off my knee. If this were a boxing match, then the news about firefighting would have been the knockout punch.

The clock on the wall ticked loudly in the suddenly silent room, as if it were counting down to detonation: *ten, nine, eight ...*

My future was blowing up all around me.

"Can we talk about the risks to Hudson?" Mom pursed her lips. "I think there's some confusion ..."

I stared at the empty square with my name underneath it and tried to ignore her.

"Okay, let's sort this out." Karen's speech was calm and steady, like a coach during a post-loss press conference. She pointed at the half-colored circle and square that represented my grandparents on the family tree. "Your grandparents are carriers. They each have one nonworking copy of the alpha-1 gene. They aren't affected like your uncle because they still have a working copy of the gene. For the child of two carriers, there is a twenty-five percent chance of inheriting two working copies of the gene, a fifty percent chance of inheriting one working copy of the gene —"

"— and being a carrier like their parents," I added.

"Yes, and a twenty-five percent chance of being affected."

"And being sick like me." I wanted to grab the pencil out of Karen's hand and fill in my square so we could get this over with.

"No, you have a twenty-five percent risk of having alpha-1. But there's a seventy-five percent chance you don't," Karen said.

"You don't have to lie to me." I pulled at the Buffalo Sabres jersey I'd worn for good luck, even though the sleeves were too short for me. "I know I'm affected. I have asthma."

Confusion spread across Karen's face. "But asthma is not part of alpha-1."

"Of course it is," I insisted. "Asthma is genetic. Alpha-1 is genetic. And they both affect the lungs."

The genetic counselor leaned forward. "Asthma is common. Alpha-1 is not common. And, yes, they both have a genetic component. But the two are not connected."

I stared at her in disbelief. "For real?"

"For real. The chance of you being affected with alpha-1 is twenty-five percent." Karen looked me in the eye as though she were begging for a truth point. "You seem like a sporty guy, so I'm going to give you an analogy."

"A what?" The switch from a science lesson to vocabulary had happened too fast — and neither one was my specialty.

"If you were betting on a game, the odds would be stacked against you being affected with alpha-1."

I let that sink in. I'd be pretty confident going into a game with only a one-in-four chance of losing. But still, nothing was ever certain until the score was final. And really, it all came down to fifty-fifty — win or lose — I either had it or I didn't. "I want to be tested, like Uncle Vic."

"Genetic testing is not simple," Mom said.

"It's just a blood test," I shot back, crossing my arms over my chest. At least some of my research was paying off.

Mom nudged my arm. "There are things to consider — like insurance."

Karen sorted through her pile of papers and pulled out a colorful, laminated pamphlet. She began to read out a list of reasons *not* to get tested: "Your ability to get health and life insurance. Genetic discrimination. Social and psychological consequences ..."

"Don't you have to tell those blood-sucking insurance dudes about family history anyway?" asked Uncle Vic.

"A positive predictive-test result gives a higher and far more definitive risk than family history. So some insurance companies might charge a higher premium because of a family history, but you can be denied insurance altogether based on a genetic test result."

"That should be illegal," Mom muttered.

Karen referred to another chart in the pamphlet. "In some cases ..."

Without listening to what she was saying, I waited for her to stop talking. I didn't want to see another chart or picture. Missing school no longer felt like a bonus — this entire appointment had been one long classroom lecture. "But Uncle Vic got tested."

"Testing people who already have symptoms can help us with treatment options and prognosis." Karen pointed at another page in the booklet. "But testing of minors without symptoms has its own set of considerations."

"So when can I get tested?"

"Not today." Karen folded her hands together and rested them on the table like a judge reviewing a case. "There is still a lot of information for your family to process and a lot of unknowns. In ten years there could be a cure for alpha-1. Or there could be information from your genetic test that we can't predict at the current time."

I could feel Mom square her shoulders, ready to tag team with Karen if necessary.

"What I need you to get from this appointment is that your chance of being affected is only twenty-five percent." Karen wrote the number down on a piece of paper and circled it. "And that most people with alpha-1 can have a very high quality of life as long as certain precautions are taken. Maybe we can introduce you to some kids who are living with alpha-1 ..."

Whatever fight I had left evaporated with the mention of other kids who already knew they had alpha-1. What would it be like to know that about yourself? Having lived my life in the dark, I'd always wanted to know more — but was it possible to know too much? I shook my head.

"So, I guess we're done for today?" said Uncle Vic.

"Do you have any more questions, Hudson?"

I shook my head again.

But Mom wasn't done. "What about these precautions? Preventative measures? Lifestyle management?"

"Mostly, it's the same as what you would do for asthma." Karen's eyes did their magical disappearing act again as a smile spread across her face. "But I'll send a letter to your general practitioner with some surveillance recommendations as well."

"So, we done here?" repeated Uncle Vic.

"Not quite," said Karen. "We still need to talk about Martha's risks."

I looked at Mom. There were tears in her eyes. My stomach turned as I realized how selfish I'd been, ignoring her feelings and thinking only of myself. Again.

"We already know that I'm a carrier," said Mom, wiping her cheek with the back of her hand. "That it's all my fault that Darwyn was affected, and now Hudson —" Her voice cracked.

"This is no more your fault than it was your mom's and dad's," Karen said gently. "Everyone inherits a few nonworking genes, and alpha-1 is one of the more common ones."

"And you only find out you're a carrier if you have kids with someone who has the same busted-up gene." I was trying to show I'd been paying attention to make Mom feel better, but as I said it, I realized I really did understand. "My dad's a carrier, too."

"Good point, kid." Uncle Vic's head swiveled back and forth between Karen and Mom. "He should be informed. He might have other kids."

I shuddered. Just when I thought I finally knew what was going on, here was another curveball. I could have a half brother or sister out there somewhere.

"Yes, he should be informed," said Karen. "For the sake of his children, but also for his own health. We know he has one nonworking copy of the alpha-1 gene, but he could have two."

"So, that would mean that he could be affected, too," said Uncle Vic.

"Hey, wait!" A thought worse than the possibility of half brothers and sisters hit me like a sucker punch. "Doesn't that mean Mom could also be affected?"

"It's unlikely, but we have to consider all possibilities," said Karen.

"I don't have any symptoms," said Mom.

"You are only thirty-five."

Mom pushed her fingers over her eyes. "Why don't you two go for a walk while Karen and I finish up?" she said to Uncle Vic.

"You sure?" Even though Uncle Vic sounded doubtful, he was already pushing himself away from the table.

"This is what I want," said Mom. "I just need to process things in my own way. We'll talk about it later." She smiled at me. "Okay?"

"Okay." I wanted to stay and support Mom, but I also wanted to respect her need for privacy. I'd been so absorbed in searching for the parent who'd left that I'd ignored the feelings of the one who'd stayed.

Uncle Vic opened the door. "Come on, kid."

"Thanks, Mom." I leaned over to give her a half hug. Her tears were gone.

"Vic, Hudson, please call or email if you have any questions," said Karen. "And we'll set a follow-up appointment in a year's time."

Scraping my knees under the desk, I awkwardly unfolded myself from the chair. As Uncle Vic and I left the room, I almost felt like a prisoner escaping a jail cell.

Except I knew that my family would never be free from alpha-1.

CHAPTER TWENTY-FOUR

When we got home, I turned on my laptop and saw a message from Willow.

Missed U @ school 2-day. CU @ the dance 2-nite

I really didn't want to go to the dance.

But I really *did* want to see Willow.

I called Trev, hoping to convince him to come with me. I figured he'd want to go to the dance about as much as he wanted to go to the dentist. But to my surprise, he said yes. Another thing I'd missed in my pathetically self-absorbed state: there was a girl he liked in his math class.

"Plus, it'll give you a chance to dance with Willow," Trev said when he was finished telling me about the math girl.

"Willow's just a friend, Trev."

"Whatever."

"And, hey, listen." Thoughts were flying at me like balls at a net during the pregame warm-up. "Have you talked to Coach yet?"

"Nope, I didn't get a chance today. Why?"

"I need to talk to him, too."

"About what?"

"About cutting me." I felt a strength inside me that I recognized, if only slightly, from my hockey days. "If it's because of my asthma, he needs to know that's not fair. I need to convince him I have what it takes." The genetic counselor had given me a second chance. Maybe Coach would, too.

"Right on." I could almost see Trev smiling through the phone.

"Do you mind if we get to the dance a bit early?"

"Why not. I'll be ready to go when you are." Trev covered the phone for a moment, and I could hear mumbling in the background. "Gran made cabbage rolls."

"I'm on my way!"

❧❧❧

I grabbed my go-to Halloween costume — a Ghostface mask — and headed downstairs. Mom and Uncle Vic were sitting in the living room, talking quietly.

"Are you heading out to trick-or-treat already?" Mom asked.

"No, there's a dance at school. Is it okay if I go?"

"Sure, but could we talk first?"

I pulled on my toque. "Trev's waiting."

"It's important." Mom patted the sofa next to her.

"Okay," I said, but I didn't sit down. The last thing I wanted to do was get trapped in another long discussion about alpha-1. I decided to make the first offensive move. "I have stuff to say, too."

I told them about being cut from basketball. About how I was going to talk to the coach.

Uncle Vic whistled. "You go, kid!"

"Good for you, Hudson." Mom smiled.

"Thanks." I turned to leave, hoping this feel-good moment had wiped out whatever she'd wanted to say.

But it hadn't. "So, you don't have any questions about today?" she asked. "About the genetic-counseling appointment?"

"Nope."

"You understand your risks?" she persisted. "What you need to do?"

"I know that there's a good chance I'm not affected. And that either way, I need to take care of my asthma." And then, to prove that I understood, I told her that I hadn't been using the peak flow meter, even though I'd been having more attacks. I did it mostly to hurry the conversation along. But I have to admit, it felt good to come clean.

As she listened to me talk, Mom looked more sad

than mad. When I was done, she said, "So we need to go see Dr. M., again."

"I guess," I said. "Sorry, Mom."

"It's okay," she said.

"I'm proud of you, kid," said Uncle Vic. "And because of you, I'm going to stop taking all those pills. Even if I need help doing it."

Embarrassment, the good kind, burned my ears. "Uh, Uncle Vic? I'm sorry I accused you of, you know —"

"Forget it, kid."

I looked down at the sofa, tracing a crack in the leather with my finger. "Can I go now?"

"What about firefighting?" asked Mom.

"We'll see." I shrugged. "There are other things I can do."

"Wow." She looked like she was about to cry for the second time that day. "That's very mature, Hudson."

I shook off the compliment, knowing that she wasn't ready to hear about the cool (but dangerous) careers E. O. had suggested. "Now can I go?"

"There's still something I want to discuss with you."

"Can it wait?" My mouth was watering for Gran's rice-and-sausage-stuffed cabbage rolls. Plus, I'd had enough of this emotional stuff for one day. Probably for the next decade.

"It's about your dad ..." Mom cleared her throat, like it wasn't possible to say his name without choking. "Josip Novak."

My heart slam-dunked to the bottom of my overgrown feet. I shoved my hands in my pockets and glanced at Uncle Vic, sitting in the armchair across from Mom.

"I don't know how to tell you this, Hudson, Vic, but ..." She folded her hands in her lap. "He's dead," she said quietly, her eyes still a bit misty.

I froze. So did Uncle Vic.

The news came as such a shock that it almost bounced right off me. I'd never really known the guy, so what did it matter that he was dead? I'd gone looking for him because it felt like something was missing. But how can you miss something you never really had?

Except ... it did matter. And not just to me, but to Mom and Uncle Vic, as well. Someone they knew — someone they'd both loved in one way or another — was gone. My dad.

As the frozen sensation wore off, pain began to creep through me. I sat down.

"I should've told you ..." Her voice trailed off

again. "I don't know why I didn't. I was trying to protect you, I guess. But since we're getting things out in the open ..."

"I don't believe it." Uncle Vic rubbed his hands up and down the tops of his legs like he was trying to start a fire.

I couldn't believe it either. I couldn't believe Mom was finally coming clean. And I couldn't believe that Uncle Vic hadn't known.

"I'll be right back." Mom stood, wobbled a little and then stumbled toward her office.

I listened to her open the drawer to her desk, followed by the closet door, and then the muffled clang of the metal filing cabinet.

"You didn't know?" I asked Uncle Vic, even though his body language made the answer more than clear.

He shook his head. "He was my best friend."

Guilt gnawed at me. Why hadn't I left well enough alone?

Mom returned, carrying a thick envelope. "I got this over the summer," she said as she dropped heavily back onto the sofa. "We'd been in touch on and off, before ..." Her eyes filled with tears. "Joe, your dad, was on the road to recovery. From his, uh, addiction."

Uncle Vic's face turned as white as my Halloween

mask. "I should've reached out. I could've helped him ..."

Should've. Could've. Wished I'd never ... Uncle Vic was doing the same thing as me — regretting everything, as if doing so would bring my dad back.

One tear escaped Mom's eye, gaining speed as it fell down her cheek and dropped off her chin. It was the only one. "The addiction center sent me the death certificate and a brief letter he wrote to each of us."

"Cause of death?" asked Uncle Vic.

"Overdose," whispered Mom. "Probably intentional."

"Suicide." Uncle Vic pulled at his goatee. "Sh — shoot."

Mom cleared her throat. "There were no assets to distribute, and the letters are sealed. I'm sorry I didn't give them to you sooner."

The color was slowly returning to Uncle Vic's unshaven cheeks. "Have you read yours?"

"No." She handed him an envelope with *Victor Pickle* scrawled on the front. "Not yet. I guess I was protecting myself, just like I was trying to protect ... I'll read it when I'm ready."

Uncle Vic took the envelope from her. "Thanks, sis."

"You should know, Hudson ..." Mom hesitated and handed me an envelope with the same scrawl. *Hudson.* "It wasn't his fault. Addiction is an illness, not a choice. And like so many diseases, it can be genetic. That's why I don't want you to get involved in drugs. Ever."

"I haven't — ever." I reached for the envelope, and for a moment, I didn't think she was going to let go. "And I won't."

"Thank you," Mom said quietly.

My heart pounded in my ears as I turned the envelope over in my hands. I felt exhausted, like I'd just finished a shorthanded shift on the ice.

"Whatever questions you have ..." Mom picked at her nails. "Please ask. I'm sure you'll want to talk about — "

"I do." I swallowed. "I will. But not now."

Mom raised her eyebrows as I handed back the envelope. "Hudson?"

It was like I'd been seeing things through a fog of craziness, but now everything suddenly became clear. "I'm not ready, either." My heart was still pounding, but my chest didn't feel tight — not at all. I had enough going on with my asthma, our family history of alpha-1 and not making the basketball team. I'd convinced myself that knowing about my dad would somehow help with all of it. Instead, it had only made things more complicated. Too complicated. I was ready to let it go. For now.

"Okay. Let me know when you are." Mom leaned over and gave me a quick kiss on the cheek. "I love you, Hudson."

"And that goes double for me, kid." Uncle Vic's letter lay in his lap. The envelope was already opened. Had Mom hid the news from Uncle Vic because she was trying to protect me or him?

"Thanks." As I said this, Willow's words came to mind, as if she were haunting me like a ghost. *Family is what you make it.*

"You better get going to that dance, kid," said Uncle Vic. "Make some girl happy with a dose of that old Pickle charm."

I felt bad leaving but, at the same time, relieved.

I was ready for some cabbage rolls at Trev's.

CHAPTER TWENTY-FIVE

When we got to the school, neither basketball coach was there. I was surprised. In elementary school, every teacher had to chaperone our silly little dances. But then again, none of those dances happened outside of regular school hours.

Strike one.

We started circling the gym. Trev's eyes scanned the crowd, searching for his math girl. "She said she was coming with friends," he grumbled. "That she'd be here by seven."

"Maybe she's in a costume that disguises who she is?" I suggested. But as I looked around the room, I knew it was unlikely. Most of the girls were dressed in skimpy outfits that didn't hide much. It was the guys who were wearing full-face masks, like me, or no costume at all, like Trev.

"Maybe." Trev sounded as unconvinced as I was.

Strike two.

Trev and I picked what we thought was a safe spot

in the corner. I barely recognized the gym. In the dark, with the spooky decorations and the thumping beat of the music, everything seemed transformed.

I spotted Willow dancing with a group of friends, each of them dressed like one of the seven dwarves. Willow, standing almost a foot taller than the rest, wore a fake white beard, a pointy red hat, a matching belted tunic and a huge grin — partly real and partly painted — on her shiny, freckled face. Happy.

I tried not to stare, but they were making quite an impression as they danced around Snow White. I wasn't the only one watching.

"Hey, look who's here. It's Mr. Kung Fu." Aidan's new nickname for Trev was a huge improvement over the flapping and clucking, especially since he said it with a degree of respect.

I wasn't so lucky. Aidan pulled down my mask. "And good ol' Wheezy."

I glanced over at Willow to see if she was watching. I didn't want her to see Aidan getting in my face — again. Aidan followed my gaze. "I have no idea what that girl sees in you."

"Me?" I croaked in surprise.

Aidan smirked as he pointed his chin to the ceiling, exaggerating our height difference. "I guess you're kind of hard to miss."

There was a friendly tone to Aidan's voice. Or, if not exactly friendly, at least a little less cruel. Still, I'd had enough of his bullying. It was time to stick up for myself. I still had a strike left. "Why don't —"

But Aidan interrupted before I had a chance to figure out what I was going to say. "I guess it's time to call a truce." He thrust his arm forward. For a second, I thought he was going to punch me in the gut. Instead, he grabbed my hand and twisted it into a thumbs-up handshake. "Since we're teammates now."

"What?"

"You better be as good as Coach thinks you are, Wheezy." There wasn't even a hint of sarcasm in Aidan's voice. "Last year the senior team went all the way to state finals."

Numb with disbelief, I pushed my mask back into place as Aidan sauntered away. Trev nudged my arm with his shoulder. The warm feeling of victory swept through me as I realized what had happened. "I only looked at the junior list," I said.

As Trev and I crossed the gym, I tried not to let myself get too excited. We scanned the senior team list, still hanging where Coach Koniuk had posted it three days ago. I couldn't believe I'd missed it — right there under *Aidan Pace* was *Hudson Pickle*. I felt like tearing the piece of paper off the wall and holding it high above my head like it was the Stanley Cup.

I'd made the team! I'd made the *senior* boys' basketball team!

I was still recovering from the shock when the music changed. I looked out over the dance floor, but I had lost sight of Willow. Did she know that I'd made the team?

Beside me, Trev was scanning the crowd as well. A frown spread across his face as he scratched his head. I'd never seen him so disappointed. I was about to ask if he wanted to split when Willow appeared in front of us.

"Come on," she said, grabbing my hand and Trev's at the same time. "This is a *dance*. You too, Trev!"

Willow dragged us across the gym until we were right in front of the DJ, in the middle of her group of friends. "Now dance!" I could see her lips move, but the words got carried away by the music.

"Nice costume," I said, leaning in close to her ear.

"Thanks for the inspiration," she said. Or at least I think that's what she said.

Talking was a waste of time, so I moved my feet back and forth, feeling self-conscious. I glanced over at Trev. His frown had disappeared and he was working the dance floor like it was the dojo. Trev could really groove — I hoped his math girl was somewhere, watching.

Willow leaned toward me and spoke right into my ear. "Move your arms, too. Like you're dribbling the ball." She flicked her hands up and down to demonstrate.

I tried to get in the zone, but it was impossible. Dancing was definitely not my sport.

"Having fun?" Willow asked when the music finally changed.

I wasn't about to tell her that I'd rather be stuffing my face with Halloween candy in celebration of my basketball success. Instead, I nodded and said, "I know I said it before, Willow, but really, congratulations on making the team."

"Congrats to you, too!" Willow looked happy enough to float. "I knew you'd make it, but I didn't know you'd make the senior team!"

The deep bass of the next song drowned out any chance of further conversation. I tried to move my hands in time with the beat the way Willow had demonstrated. But instead of being smooth and natural like Trev, I felt like I was doing the chicken dance.

I finally started to relax when a song Uncle Vic

had shared with me came on. It was a bit slower, but not too slow. My dancing still sucked, but at least I wasn't flapping my wings anymore. Willow gave me the thumbs-up. I shrugged and did an exaggerated butt wiggle just for fun. I didn't care if I looked like a dork — I liked to hear Willow laugh.

The music stopped and Willow was still laughing. Not at me, but with me.

After a few more songs, Trev caught my eye and made a motion toward the door with his head.

"We're going to split," I said to Willow quickly, before another song drowned me out. "But listen, can I call you sometime? So we can talk about ... stuff?"

"Of course." She pulled me into a hug, fast and tight. I could feel her breath on my neck for a moment, and then it was gone. "I'll call you tomorrow," she said as she let go.

Walking across the gym with Trev, I didn't even try to wipe the happiness from my face. Because for the first time since I'd started junior high, I was happy. Truly happy.

From the top of my head, right down to my Pickle genes.